Beanstock

-MURDER AT PARSLEY MANOR-

AF176627

Butler Beanstock investigates
The first case

facebook: A.W. Benedict
instagram: @awbenedict_autorin
Website: awbenedict.de

translation: Ute Hieksch

cover design: www.wolf-photoart.de

font design: Tobias Wieduwilt

management: Chris Wieduwilt

proofreading: SchriftWerk - Jona Gellert

© 2023
Manufacturing and Publishing: BoD – Books on Demand, Norderstedt.
ISBN 9783756862115

Bibliographic information from the German National Library:
The German National Library lists this publication in the Deutsche
Nationalbibliografie;
detailed bibliographic data is available on the Internet

Beanstock

-MURDER AT PARSLEY MANOR-

"Old sins cast long shadows"

Agatha Christie

Appointment with Death

"What a waste of my precious time," the old lady muttered as the loud staccato of her cane echoed on the pavement along West Street. Astonished pedestrians walked past her, shaking their heads in disdain as they made their way to the neighbouring restaurants and bars after their theatre visit.

St Martin's Theatre had been filled to capacity. A play by the popular crime writer Agatha Christie always guaranteed a full house – as well as a full box office – for its theatre owner, who undoubtedly entertained the notion of Mrs. Christie's "The Mousetrap" also gracing his stage someday soon.

At the end of the fourth curtain, the charming and diminutive impresario rubbed his hands, visibly satisfied. He stroked his shiny, pomaded hair, wound his white scarf around his neck, and blithely whistled as he left the theatre towards the Red Backdrop bar in West Street, which was a very popular establishment among the theatre crowd.

The only person who appeared utterly displeased was old Miss Agatha Eugenie Hillman. Her solicitor's office had given her the play ticket, and cheerfully brought to her attention that the author of the play, *Appointment with Death*, had the same first name as the office's esteemed client.

But at that pivotal moment Mr. Pridges, solicitor at Pington, Pington and Pridges, had suddenly realised the theatre ticket had not been a good idea at all and that flowers might have been a more appropriate choice.

He was already acquainted with the old woman and her idiosyncrasies by virtue of his office's representation of the Hillman family inheritance case. But Miss Agatha Eugenie Hillman – case number 5/30/47, succession case of Hillman, Parsley Field – was an excellent client in terms of monetary value and therefore extremely beneficial to the office. For this reason he had overlooked her minor quirks.

Agatha Eugenie Hillman was a tall, gaunt, 65-year-old woman. She wore her thin grey hair in a topknot on a small head perched atop her long, wrinkled neck, accompanied by a perennially pinched facial expression reminiscent of a shrivelled potato. Her ice-blue eyes seemed cold and unrelenting, and her thin lips appeared to have never learned to smile; they were always pursed tightly like a frightened child in the dentist's chair.

Her housemaid Polly liked her about as much as hail in August, a sentiment the pretty Polly had whispered behind her employer's back to the greengrocer's messenger boy. The phrase had spread like wildfire and never failed to amuse the old lady's numerous deliverymen.

On this day, Friday November 1947, the old lady – impeccably attired in her best dress of fine black lace and a red fox coat from the prestigious *House of Redfox* company in London – had set out for St Martin's Theatre.

The taxi Polly hailed brought them to West Street. Upon their arrival Miss Hillman was already complaining at the theatre entrance, claiming that the seat assigned to her was completely inappropriate. But upon checking her ticket and surveying the theatre filled to capacity, she had been informed otherwise, whereupon the old lady, snorting with rage, limped to her seat in the ninth row.

By the end of the first act, she had not stopped loudly pontificating to her seatmates about the implausibility of this purely fabricated story. Poor Mr Plumm on her right was too polite to say anything, whereas Mrs Karmikle, the feisty lady to her left, told Miss Hillman in no uncertain terms during the intermission that she should either keep her opinions to herself or leave, and that she would be only too happy to arrange a taxi on her behalf. Suffice it to say, during the rest of the performance Miss Hillmann was somewhat quieter.

The old lady now stood outside the theatre, grumbling to herself while looking around for a taxi. She spotted one across the street and approached it.

The taxi driver was deeply engrossed in his newspaper.

Miss Hillman noisily rapped on the window with her cane as a ploy to garner attention. The taxi driver rolled down the window and scowled at her.

"Hey, lady, what are you playing at? Do you want to pay for a new window? What's your problem, anyway?"

"Stop babbling, it's obvious I need a taxi. Come on, open the door." The taxi driver was too surprised to think of a suitable rejoinder. He stepped out of his vehicle, opened the back door and ushered the lady in.

"Number 10 A Cornwall Gardens. And make it snappy. Come on! What are you waiting for?" The taxi driver was lucky that the lady did not hear him muttering under his breath. He started the engine as quickly as possible and turned the next corner at a speed that abruptly jolted her in the back seat. Fifteen minutes later he stopped in front of house number 10, which was quite a triumph amid the evening traffic. But Miss Hillman did not regard the journey as such, of course. She stepped out of the vehicle, handed him the requisite fare without any tip, leaned on her cane as she limped towards the entrance of her house and grumbled all the while about today's exorbitant taxi fares.

The houses in Cornwall Gardens had been a resplendent white before the war, complete with columns in front, beautiful overhead balconies and wrought iron paling fences next to the entrance.

But the facades had since taken on a grey pallor and rust was forming on the wrought iron. Identical houses built side by side might seem prosaic to some, yet it was precisely this design concept that rendered the city's Cornwall Gardens residential area so appealing. Kensington as a whole was the preferred residential district of the rich and upper class. The neighbourhood was replete with delicatessens, whose offerings were finally beginning to look slightly more enticing again after the end of the Great War.

Miss Hillman could now afford whatever her heart desired. She clumsily took the key out of her pearl-studded handbag, unlocked the door, entered a spacious vestibule and then turned on the light next to the door. A dimly flickering ceiling lamp illuminated the room.

The old lady looked at the lamp above her with narrowed eyes, shook her head and groused, "When will those lazybones from the gas company actually do a proper job? The war is long over." Then she turned around laboriously and emphatically locked the front door again.

"What a bloody waste of my time, that play was utterly ridiculous", she said aloud into the silence of the house. "Murdered with a syringe outside a tent. Very funny, indeed. What are the odds... Now I know why I don't read those insufferable mystery novels.

And to add insult to injury, I have to prepare tea on my own now because this feckless girl needs a day off. Utterly ridiculous."

She took off her red fox coat and limped into the kitchen while leaning on her cane. To her surprise, a tray with a pot topped by a tea cosy and a covered plate of sandwiches had been placed on the counter. The girl had certainly never done anything like this before – or had she?

"I guess all the pains I took to turn her into a proper housemaid have finally paid off", the old lady muttered. She tasted one of the sandwiches and poured herself a cup of tea.

"This is certainly not what I'd call a proper sandwich; it's as dry as a rusk." She took the mug and stomped into the fireplace parlour while angrily striking the floor with her cane.

"At least she had the wherewithal to make a fire before she left."

The old lady sat down in the wing chair in front of the fireplace and noisily sipped her tea. After a short time she felt warm and sleepy.

"I never forget. Remember that. I've never forgotten anything, not an action, not a name, not a face. . ."[1] Agatha Eugenie was taken aback. She had definitely not imagined those words. The whispered words came from a dark corner behind her.

"Who's there, what are you doing in my house?

---

[1] Excerpt of Agatha Christie's "Appointment with Death"

Polly, is that you?" she asked somewhat frantically. The voice sounded again.

"Agatha, you know it's Polly's day off. At this very moment she is enjoying the company of a very nice young man and splitting her sides laughing at your expense again. Don't worry, my dear, I'm not one of those ghosts who haunted Ebenezer Scrooge. Besides, we both know that this particular story would end poorly, featuring you in the starring role. No, in your case, the story would end with the ghost of Christmas Eves to come and a tombstone bearing your name. Because you will never change, nor do I ever expect you to."

Agatha was too tired to stand up, and all of a sudden, her legs did not want to cooperate. Moreover, she couldn't even utter a single word from her dry lips. What on earth was happening to her?

"Well, Agatha, don't try so hard. There was just a trace of something extra in the tea which will only make you feel slightly tired. Besides, I want to have a chat with you for a moment. And I gather you heard that sentence I just quoted earlier from the play, didn't you?"

"What does that dreadful play have to do with it?"

Agatha's voice now sounded hoarse and croaky as she made a valiant effort to utter even a single word.

"This wonderful play by Agatha Christie has a very crucial role, my dear. It's truly amazing how the author could centre a plot on punishing a woman who

11

has brought nothing but anguish to the people around her. The kind of person who flits about like an evil spirit and derives joy from hurting people until they die a gruesome death, solely for her own gratification. Isn't that alone worth a special type of punishment? Tell me, Agatha Eugenie Hillman. Haven't you already unleashed enough misery upon your fellow humans? Your comeuppance merely entails a small step, which will soon be over and done with."

The old woman felt a sting on her arm.

"It's so easy. You receive an injection of digitoxin each day for your heart problems, just like the woman in Mrs Christie's brilliant play. Furthermore, you've been constantly insulting the kind soul of a nurse who administers your daily injection. Oh, Agatha, how foolish of you. She will tell Scotland Yard that you've been a terrible patient, always caustic and stubborn. As a consequence it wouldn't come as a surprise if you unintentionally overdosed, after all, you might have felt poorly tonight. Did you know, my dear, that digitoxin is extracted from the highly toxic red foxglove? You didn't? You really should read more, it's a wonderfully educational pursuit. Oh, how silly of me to forget: you don't read, that's no good at all. Reading is like eating. It is essential for survival. You don't understand this concept? Don't worry. I can assure you that you will likely never read anything now that you haven't ever deigned to previously read.

Yet I feel rather sorry for Polly. She will be forced to find a new job. But don't worry, my dear, she will most certainly be in demand, she's still young and has a pretty face."

And then a soft chuckle could be heard. The shadow behind Agatha moved towards the wing chair. A log was thrown into the fire.

"I'll make sure your room is warm and cosy, it's the least I can do." A hand gently grasped the old lady's wrist.

"I'm still talking yet you haven't been paying any attention at all. Have a pleasant flight to *hell*, Agatha Eugenie Hillman."

The shadow slipped back into the darkness and after a short time a door could be heard clicking shut in the distance.

Then everything fell silent in the house at 10 A Cornwall Gardens. A small mouse left its hiding place and tentatively surveyed the room. Until now, there had been voices and the dreadful clacking of a cane on the floor tiles, which the little mouse had not at all appreciated, for fear its ears would end up tangled in a knot. But now there was only dead silence in the house.

The little mouse carefully scurried into the kitchen, past the mousetrap, which it had already discovered a long time ago and which was to be avoided at any cost.

What silly notions these people conjure up. Do

they really think small animals are less intelligent than humans?

The enticing aroma of bread and cheese rose up from the kitchen counter. The mouse quickly climbed up and then back down on the floor with a piece of cheese. The house was still silent save for the sound of the little rodent's scurrying on the tiles. The little mouse ran further into the living room where it was much warmer. A pleasant fire was blazing away in the fireplace.

The little mouse ran to the big wing chair in front of it and looked up. It was so frightened that the last bite of cheese almost fell out of its mouth. That abominable, old, loud woman was sitting there. But she wasn't moving.

The mouse sniffed around. Its alert animal instincts soon detected that this terrible housemate would never set a mousetrap for it again.

The mouse would have likely smiled, if it were able.

It quietly scampered back to the kitchen and gobbled up the tasty sandwiches on the counter. What a glorious evening!

Parsley Manor

The needle made a soft crackling sound as it hit the thick shellac record. The slow and measured melody gradually rose.

The man moved to the rhythm of the music in front of the small round mirror on the wall. His right hand deftly scratched his cheek with the razor. Every now and then he would pause, close his eyes with pleasure and hum quietly.

The house slowly awoke as the sun was rising outside the window. The noise from the record served to wake up the inhabitants of the upper floor in the old, stately mansion. Complaints about the morning noise were already piling up on housekeeper Mrs Argyle's walnut bureau. There would surely be another short note this week to this effect. The noise complaint notes were primarily issued by Filomena Arbuckle, the lady of the manor's maid, who in turn received it via the feisty cook Mrs Porkpie, who had received it from the chauffeur Gonzales – who always punctuated his objections with a curt *maldita* – and via the servant Harrison beforehand. Everyone signed the little note, regardless that they realised full well that nothing would ever change.

However, the gardener Herringbone never signed, as he felt very fortunate to live with his insolent cat, Mortecai, in a separate room next to the glass greenhouse. When Mrs Porkpie again secretly informed him about the latest attack on her auditory nerves during breakfast, he simply smiled and thoughtfully stroked his bushy moustache.

Butler Arthur Reginald Beanstock was untouchable, since he enjoyed his lordship's complete trust and as long as that lordship did not hear any of the purported noise, the little notes would ultimately disappear in the walnut bureau and, at most, garner a raised eyebrow by way of any reaction.

Mrs Argyle had arrived at Parsley Manor to begin her position as a housekeeper shortly after the butler Beanstock. She was the only one who witnessed the kind, empathic nature of the butler's personality. When she had made his acquaintance many years ago, she was struggling to cope with a bad experience, which was the reason she had to leave London and take the job in the countryside with the Baronets Parsley. The butler had treated her with a great deal of decorum and sympathy, which she would never forget.

Beanstock regarded his clean-shaven face in the mirror. He took the towel, wiped the last traces of foam from his cheek and reached for the comb. He carefully smoothed back his full head of black hair.

Stroke by stroke, he achieved the butler aesthetic his employer preferred: no beard, a dazzling white, freshly starched shirt with a stand-up collar and a black tie, black trousers with pleats, a black jacket and a black waistcoat.

Beanstock's wardrobe comprised several identical garments as well as a black tailcoat for festive occasions. He did not own any casual garments. Moreover, a casual appearance outside of his duties did not seem appropriate to him.

The music selection ended with a furious drum roll. He carefully lifted the tone arm from the old record, placed the turntable back into its wooden case and closed the front flap adorned with wonderful coloured inlay. He turned the small gold key in the lock and put it in his right waistcoat pocket as he did every morning. His finger tapped the pocket three times. Satisfied, he nodded.

There is nothing more conducive to the perfect execution of tasks ahead than a balanced morning routine. Beanstock was ready.

He needed this morning ritual which had accorded him strength and satisfaction during his 20-year service to Baronet Sir Percival Parsley. A quiet knock sounded at his room door.

The butler cleared his throat to make his voice sound even-tempered and briefly responded, "Come in." The housemaid Bernice stood in the doorway with a small wooden tray, curtsied and angrily looked at the butler.

"Your morning tea, Sir."

Beanstock noticed she had overemphasised the word, "Sir".

The young girl with rosy cheeks and bright, expressive eyes looked at him expectantly. She had long reddish hair tied back in a braid.

Her dark green calf-length dress had long, tight sleeves with white cuffs, over which she wore a white apron with wide straps reaching down to her back.

Beanstock pointed to the round table next to his armchair by way of instruction.

"Thank you, Bernice."

The maid curtsied again and walked out the door.

Beanstock drank his morning cup of tea – Darjeeling, half a teaspoon of sugar, two spoons of milk – in his room at 6:30 a.m. every day without fail.

Between 6:00 a.m. and 7:00 a.m., the staff of Parsley Manor had sufficient time to complete their morning toilet, tidy their rooms and have breakfast. The butler arrived in the kitchen at exactly 7:00 a.m. and allocated the day's duties together with Mrs Argyle the housekeeper.

While Parsley Manor was not the largest mansion in the area around the small village of Parsley Field, it was certainly a sight to behold. Built in the Elizabethan style of architecture, it was E-shaped and constructed from reddish sandstone.

An ivy-covered entrance porch adorned the centre at the front of the building, whereas a spacious terrace with a wide staircase to the garden and gravelled paths leading to the glass greenhouse had been constructed at the back.

Imposing vertically and horizontally split windows dominated the facade, which extended to both floors in the entrance hall. Surrounded by shady orchards, a walled vegetable and herb garden as well as lavish flower beds, the house was reminiscent of an enchanted fairytale castle.

An ancient, huge ginkgo tree was located in the square in front of the entrance and was the favourite of the lady of the manor, Lady Fedora Parsley. She was a feisty little lady, her round, rosy face always smiling. The few white strands in her dark blond hair didn't seem to bother her at all. On most occasions she could be seen wearing a large light straw hat, her painting utensils in tow, as she ambled across the spacious garden on the quest for a worthwhile subject. She had been painting flowers for many years with great success and had already received numerous accolades. Her publications were well known and popular throughout the country.

Several years ago, her husband Sir Percival Parsley had fulfilled a dream of his by modernising what he had called the old, draughty masonry. In addition to the extensive renovations and expansion Sir Percival had erected a beautiful Victorian-style greenhouse for his wife. This greenhouse gave Lady Fedora the idea of painting flowers. Although she had always painted stunning pictures, she attained great success from her books.

When the house was finally completed in 1939, the terrible harbingers of war were already apparent.

Sir Percival and many of the male staff had had to leave, yet not all of them had returned. But now, in 1950, life was gradually returning to normal and the Baronets could finally enjoy their country life to the fullest.

They had not lavishly set up their household, as was customary in the manors of this region. They leased the neighbouring land and lived contentedly on rental monies and income from Lady Fedora's manifold pursuits.

The dark, musty furniture had been removed and replaced by an inviting entrance hall with shiny parquet flooring and comfortable armchairs at its centre in front of a bright marble fireplace. On the left, a large white door led into the library which was both Sir Percival's favourite room and study. He spent hours there, brooding over archival material and indulging his passion by checking the local legends and sagas for their degree of authenticity.

The salon, comfortably furnished with sofas and armchairs, was located on the right side. In front of the tall windows, flocks of colourful birds adorned the patterned curtains. A wide passageway led from the salon into the music room. Although no one could actually play, a huge grand piano held court in the middle of the room. Numerous small and large framed photographs of the widespread Baronets of Parsley family had been randomly placed on the shiny black piano lid.

Next to the fireplace in the hall, a door on the left side led to the family's large dining room with a long dark oak table, upholstered chairs and huge candelabra above the table. This monstrosity was the only remaining fixture from the old furnishings. At the back of the room, tall white doors provided access to the garden and terrace. As the room was very large, the couple usually took their meals at a round table in the cosy salon.

To the right side of the hall's fireplace, a wide marble staircase led to the family's bedroom on the first floor. Lady Fedora's studio had been established there, affording a view of the garden. The distinct scent of the various paints was discernible in the hallway. Oil paints, tempera and watercolours were piled up in wide wooden drawers while hundreds of drawing pencils, charcoal pieces and brushes crowded several ceramic pots.

Wide cupboards with narrow drawers full of drawing paper were set up along the wall. Lady Fedora's drawing table was situated in front of the large window, while her numerous published flower books were prominently displayed on a shelf.

The guest rooms were located on the other side of this floor. At the bottom of the stairs, a double-wing door led to the back of the house, which mainly accommodated the kitchen area for Mrs Porkpie, the cook.

The staff's working space was also directly accessible from the staff rooms on the first floor by way of a stone stairway with a beautiful old wooden balustrade.

Next to a large modern kitchen, there was a cold storage room, a pantry, the housekeeper's office, the butler's office and a room for ironing along with a sink and cupboards full of everything the housemaid or the lady of the manor's maid might need: from sewing utensils and shoe cleaning set to stain remover, mothballs, candles, starch, silver polish and the medicine cabinet.

There was also a room where the staff took their meals. A lamp with a broad, white lampshade above a beautiful, brightly polished wooden table hung in the middle. The table was situated in front of a large window which granted a view into the orchard. Bright sunlight flooded the room by early morning. Comfortable wooden chairs with woven seats encircled the table.

A clearly visible round clock hung in a dark wooden box on the wall. Every morning it was the housekeeper's duty to wind up this clock and ensure that it displayed the exact time.

After a quick glance at the pocket watch in his waistcoat, Mr. Beanstock made his way to the staff quarters with purposeful strides. It was 7:00 a.m.; the staff were awaiting their instructions.

The butler entered the room and the din of excited voices immediately fell silent. Mrs Argyle cleared her throat and respectfully greeted the butler with a nod. The full staff complement was present, which Mr Beanstock always appreciated.

Despite the butler's and housekeeper's concerns, the Baronets had decided to employ a bare minimum of staff. They decided there needn't be an overwhelming number of subservient ghosts scurrying around the house all day. The lord of the manor had articulated his sentiments as such, and they had thus far gotten along splendidly with this arrangement.

Since the Baronets of Parsley did not have children, there was no need for a nanny, a wet nurse or a governess. Only the small assemblage of nieces and nephews briefly descended on the estate during summer vacation, as a rule.

Sir Percival eschewed enlisting a personal valet; he felt he was old enough to dress himself.

As a consequence, the servants were relegated to only the essentials and strangely enough, they all got along fine. Only during spring cleaning and for larger parties did the housekeeper, Mrs Argyle, insist on hiring additional staff.

Housekeeper Mrs Argyle, as usual, sat bolt-upright in her high-necked black dress and tightly tied back coiffed grey hair. Seated next to her at the large table was the lady of the house's maid, Filomena Arbuckle, whose hair was once again not styled according to household protocol, as Beanstock noticed. Among the staff, the housemaid Bernice and the servant Harrison, a taciturn man with ginger hair and very large, strong hands, were also present. On the other side of the table next to the housekeeper, cook Mrs Porkpie wearing a shiny white starched bonnet had taken a seat. She appeared visibly gladdened by the highly praised dishes she had lovingly prepared. By contrast, scullery maid Phillis, seated next to the plump cook, was small and nondescript with her short mousy brown hair, drab grey dress and white apron.

Sitting beside the scullery maid was the gardener, Mr Herringbone, who was grinning happily and tugging at his impressive, well-groomed moustache. The seat beside him was occupied by the tall chauffeur Gonzales, a Spaniard who appeared as a character straight out of a trashy novel with his curly jet-black hair and a perpetual mischievous smile on his sensuous lips.

Beanstock looked around and sat down opposite the housekeeper.

"Good morning", he greeted the attentive audience.

The only one still grinning was the gardener.

Phillis rose and disappeared into the kitchen for a short moment. She returned with a plate which she put down in front of the butler, as was her custom every morning. The meal comprised some porridge, a teaspoonful of sugar and a chopped apple. Phillis sat down again, smoothing her apron in the process. Beanstock gave her a brief nod as a show of gratitude. Before having his meal, he retrieved his little black book from the inside pocket of his jacket and opened it.

Every morning he started his instructions with the gardener.

"Herringbone, the flowers in the salon and the hall need to be replaced: Her Ladyship currently prefers gillyflowers. On Friday, Sir and Lady Parsley are receiving guests from London, and less fragrant flowers are in order for dinner in the dining room and the two guest rooms. I will leave the choice of flowers to you."

Beanstock did not expect an answer.

The instructions were merely routine: everybody knew what was expected of them.

"Gonzales, Sir Percival is expected to attend the clerical meeting in the village this afternoon at 4:00 p.m. Tomorrow is Thursday and her Ladyship has deigned to go shopping in London for the festive reception on Saturday. The car will be ready at 10:00 a.m."

Beanstock leafed through his book. "Now for the kitchen staff instructions: sandwiches for lunch today, and for dinner later cream of asparagus soup, lamb, a seasonal salad and semolina flummery will be served as discussed. I am sure you have already prepared the meal. You have previously received your instructions for the reception on Saturday." Beanstock turned a page of his book.

"Harrison, the fireplace in the blue guest room is not working properly. Take care of it and try not to leave the place in shambles this time.

Bernice, you can assist him and make a point of tending to it afterwards. Then you can prepare the guest rooms. We need two rooms, the blue one and the green one."

"Mrs Argyle, the two expected guests will arrive at the station on Friday at 6:00 p.m. They are friends of the Lord and Ladyship, one is Her Ladyship's publisher, Mr Van Horton, while the other is Miss Inga Hillman."

The butler paused for a moment so as not to blurt out an inappropriate comment. The housekeeper finished the butler's commentary.

"On these days the table will be set in the dining room. Mr. Beanstock will of course be responsible for the wines and spirits."

She shot a reprimanding look at Phillis. The scullery maid had giggled after whispering something to Mrs Porkpie, and in response the cook likewise giggled.

It was no secret that Miss Hillman was a celebrated actress currently filming the remake of *The House of Lady Applequeis* for Hollywood in the London studios and preferred a most unconventional lifestyle. In the past she had lived in the nearby region. Her parents had been friends with Sir Percival and Lady Fedora, and Inga, whose baptismal name was Priscilla, was Lady Fedora's godchild.

Beanstock shut the small book and carefully put it in his jacket. Then he surveyed the room.

"Thank you. If there are no more questions...? You know what to do."

Chairs were moved and everyone resumed their duties.

The cook prepared breakfast for both the lord and the lady of the manor. The maid ironed a blouse. Herringbone, grinning as usual, headed for the greenhouse. Bernice and Harrison fetched buckets and brushes. Phillis, the scullery maid, set the table in the salon.

Mrs Argyle went to her office to place orders for the celebratory welcome event, whereas Gonzalez pinched Bernice's cheek, which he did every morning, and whistled a tune on his way to the garage.

Beanstock picked up a spoon and ate his porridge slowly and pensively. After he had finished his breakfast, the postman, Mr Partridge, knocked on the back door as he did almost every morning at that time. Phillis let him in and greeted him exuberantly with a hug.

Beanstock loudly cleared his throat.

Phillis took a step back, picked up the mail and handed him a pile of letters ready for mailing.

The postman winked at her again and returned to his bicycle.

"Phillis, even if he is your father, you have to behave appropriately here. This means no displays of affection in the duty area."

"Yes, Mr Beanstock, please accept my apologies. It won't happen again."

She put the mail on the sideboard, curtsied and then returned to her duties in the kitchen.

The butler sifted through the mail. The staff mail comprised a sole letter for Mrs Argyle and a colourful postcard from Africa for the maid Filomena. The butler sorted the remaining mail into letters for Lady Fedora and Sir Percival and placed them on a silver tray next to the newspaper.

He pursed his lips upon noticing the incongruous wrinkles on the paper. But Sir Percival had instructed him to stop ironing any such wrinkles. Until a year ago it had been his morning task to smooth all correspondence in the ironing room. Then Bernice took over this task for a short time, as Beanstock had an assignment in London to carry out on behalf of Sir Percival.

The catastrophe occurred precisely on those two days. Bernice simply lacked any experience in ironing newspapers properly. She either left the iron on the paper for too long or not long enough.

Be that as it may, a crumpled – and worse – partly charred newspaper twice ended up on the breakfast table. Sir Percival had missed the daily report on the harvest progress in Parsley Field due to the holes burnt into the paper at precisely these most important parts.

This year's ___ ato ...vest w.... qu... ...ine, was all Sir Percival had managed to read.

After the butler's return from London, Sir Percival decided he no longer wanted the newspapers to be ironed. How had this impacted Beanstock's daily duties? He felt ill for days back then. Although Bernice had profusely apologised, he was inconsolable after such a faux pas.

The first lesson Beanstock had learned at butler school was how to properly iron the morning newspaper. It was both a necessity and a comforting ritual: a necessity because it made it easier for the lordship to read the paper in the morning, and a comforting ritual as Beanstock could aptly prepare for the day's duties during these silent moments.

Fortunately, he still had his morning music.

He smiled slightly at the mere thought.

Furthermore, Mr. Beanstock indulged in another passion: he had an affinity for mystery novels. There was a considerable collection in his room and if he had time, he would go to the widow Bloom's shop to pick up a new book he had ordered. Such a day usually ended late – or even early the next morning. He did not stop reading until the murderer or robber had been convicted, made notes in his little book and often realised that he knew more than the investigating detective within the first few pages.

How he loved these brainteasers.

The butler looked at the clock on the wall, grabbed the silver tray and headed for the salon. A large mirror next to the door to the entrance hall allowed a last glimpse of what he hoped was deemed correct attire and hairstyle. Before the butler could open the door, it flew open and Phillis appeared with a silver pitcher in her hand. Visibly startled, she was forced to quickly grab the pitcher with her other hand; otherwise, it would have fallen on the floor.

Beanstock shook his head rebukingly.

"You shouldn't run Phillis, do you not realise how quickly a terrible mishap could happen? Consider yourself lucky to work for such an extremely lenient employer."

Phillis blushed, curtsied and went on her way.

As Beanstock stepped into the hall, he could already hear Lady Fedora's bright cheerful voice in the salon. He entered the room with a purposeful stride, bowed slightly, handed the newspaper to Sir Percival and then placed the mail for Lady Fedora beside her seat.

"Good morning, Milady, Sir Percival!"

Beanstock bowed again.

"Morning, Beanstock!" Sir Percival replied in his loud, imposing voice. Partway under the table, the rump of a beagle was visible. The dog felt disturbed from his morning nap when he heard his master's loud voice. He lifted his head and softly whimpered before going back to sleep.

"Do you always have to shout like that, Darling? Everyone can hear you. Poor Junior. Good morning, Beanstock. Is everything prepared for Friday?"

Sir Percival guffawed loudly, as usual, which caused the ancestral portraits on the walls to start swaying. Nothing his beloved wife said would ever embarrass him.

"Everything will be properly carried out to your exacting standards, Milady. We will prepare the blue and green guest rooms. Arrangements for the dinner on Friday have already been made and Miss Hillman's reception will be on schedule. Invitations have been given to the postman. Gonzales will be at your disposal to take you to London tomorrow at 10:00 a.m. And might I also remind you of the monthly clerical meeting at 2:00 this afternoon? Sir Percival's attendance is expected." With these words he looked at his employer, expecting a groan by way of a response.

"Darling, since you are the Baronet of Parsley,

and thus steeped in family tradition, it is part of your duties. When you were conscripted to that terrible war, I took on these duties and believe me, it wasn't easy for me either. But not because I didn't enjoy these duties, but because the gentlemen in the church council were loath to having a woman attending the meetings."

Sir Percival's woebegone facial expression was clearly an attempt to garner pity from Beanstock. He had heard this story from his wife more than once. It had certainly annoyed Lady Fedora to be met with disrespect, but this all happened years ago and she still could not get over it.

"Milady fared impressively well during those tumultuous years and made a lasting impression on the parish church council", Beanstock responded in an attempt to restore marital harmony.

Lady Fedora again smiled charmingly and turned her attention to her letters. Sir Percival looked gratefully at his butler: they both knew this point of contention would repeat itself.

Back then, Lady Fedora had threatened the church council with severe consequences if they continued to underestimate her. She kept details of the situation at hand to herself and in fact had only hinted that her suggestions had fallen on deaf ears and she had been treated as if her presence in the council was purely decorative.

As a result, she had threatened to no longer

participate in the annual *Parsley Field Flowers Cup* with her books along with her prizewinning flowers. The councillors were fully aware that numerous people from other regions of Britain only travelled to this festival every year on account of Lady Fedora. The small community generated substantial revenue from these visitors. No matter whether they spent it at the widow Bloom's golf hotel and farming supplies shop or at O'Donoghue's pub, the town profited greatly during that festival week.

At that very moment while Sir Percival and Lady Fedora were absorbed in their newspaper and letters, Beanstock shuddered as Phillis barged in with a new pot of fresh tea, almost tripping over Junior, but fortunately regained her balance, anticipating her third reprimand today. At that same moment, postman Mr Partridge had crossed the stone bridge over the River Shirty and began his daily post delivery.

A Bottle of Burgundy,

a Potted Plant,

a Pasty and a Fountain Pen

The morning was going by very quickly.

Sir Percival was poring over a tricky folk tale in the library, according to which a monster had risen from the sea, spewing fire and brimstone which burned down the monastery at Parsley Field. In an ancient chronicle from the 15 th century, the monster was described as a formidable, hirsute man who was purported to have had a bull's head, two thick, pointed horns on both sides of his head as well as metal hands and feet.

Sir Percival was quite sure that this vivid description referred to the Vikings and wondered whether the Normans or the Vikings had destroyed the monastery. He was very determined to find the answer. That is, unless that damned clerical meeting interfered with his plans. A knock on the door abruptly snapped him out of his reverie.

"Yes, come on in", Sir Percival roared in his usual manner. Junior quietly yelped again. The butler entered the library with a cup of tea.

"Your tea, Sir. Now I would like to inspect the wine cellar and replenish the supplies, if necessary, upon your consent" Sir Percival was already engrossed in his book again and was only half listening.

"Beanstock, you are definitely equal to the task on your own. I know I can rely on you. Go ahead." He waved his hand dismissively, absently reached for his cup of tea and continued to read intently.

Beanstock bowed slightly and left the library. A door under the wide staircase led into the wine cellar in which Mrs Porkpie's preserved delicacies were also kept. Long rows of jars of succulent fruit, sweet jams, sour pickles and spicy chutneys were stored here, all waiting to be served.

The wine racks had been set up at the back of the high vaulted cellar. The vessels were neatly sorted into red and white wines, simple country wines as well as French wines from Gascony, which Milady preferred. A separate cabinet housed an array of exquisitely rare wines of which the Lord was very proud, such as a red 1929 Chateau Lafite Rothschild. Next to it were a few bottles of champagne, various wines, whisky and sherry. Beanstock glanced at the thermometer and was satisfied; there was no need to order additional beverages.

He turned off the light switch next to the door, left the cellar and was back in the hall again. Where was that noise suddenly coming from? Something was wrong. He headed for the kitchen area from where excited voices could be heard. He could recognise Mrs Porkpie's loud scolding and another person's distinct sobbing and wailing. He ran faster than usual towards the noise in order to stop it as quickly as possible.

In the cold storage room, the cook stood with her wooden spoon raised high and was wildly gesticulating with it in Phillis' face, which was the source of the loud snivelling. Mrs Argyle was not present, but presumably upstairs in the house checking the setup of the guest rooms. Although the butler tried to wrest the spoon away from the cook, he wasn't immediately successful.

"What is going on here, ladies? I expect an answer immediately. Your noise can be heard all the way down to the hall. This is unacceptable."

The cook struggled to regain her composure.

"One of my best pasty creations has disappeared. I made it especially for Miss Priscilla because I remembered she was crazy about it as a child. It took me a long time to make. Besides, who else except this little sweet tooth here could have taken it…?"

Phillis again started to wail and snivel. The butler took a white handkerchief out of his jacket pocket and handed it to the scullery maid. Beanstock realised from the trumpeting sounds emanating from Phillis' nose that this handkerchief would be lost forever. She wanted to return it to him, but he refused with a wry smile.

"Keep it, girl. What do you have to say for yourself regarding these accusations?"

"It wasn't me! But I'm the one who always gets blamed." Tears again rolled down her cheeks.

At that moment the gardener Mr Herringbone appeared in the outer doorway carrying an empty ceramic pot.

"Someone has stolen my Moonlight Shadow rose", he explained breathlessly. His grey tomcat Mortecai wound his way between Herringbone's legs.

The animal likely wanted to take advantage of the brouhaha to quickly sneak into the storage supply room. But of course Mortecai had no chance since Beanstock was pointing his finger at him reprovingly. Herringbone took the animal in his arms.

"Am I being accused of this as well?!" Phillis bellowed between sobs, eliciting uncomprehending stares from the gardener.

Things were starting to get interesting.

Somebody in the hall was ringing for the butler. With a gesture towards the small group in the kitchen he instructed them to wait for his return. He then briefly adjusted his garments in front of the mirror and entered the hall where Lady Fedora was standing, along with her painting utensils, visibly upset.

"Beanstock, can you imagine – my best gold fountain pen has disappeared. How can I write without my talisman? It's absolutely impossible." She was beside herself as she looked around searchingly.

The curious faces of the kitchen group appeared behind the door to the staff wing.

"My wonderful pasty, the cultivated rose and now Milady's pen. What else is going to disappear?" the cook asked quietly. Beanstock looked at her reprimandingly.

Lady Fedora was horrified.

"Sort it out, my dearest Beanstock, otherwise I'm afraid I'll be forced to stop writing forever."

The butler turned around and waved the group back into the kitchen.

"Show me where you stored the pasty, Mrs Porkpie."

The cook opened the door to the cold storage room and pointed to one of the shelves. Beanstock carefully looked around the room before he inspected the floor, on which unusual traces of dirt were visible.

Shaking her head, the cook crossed her arms as she observed him. "Where is the bottle of Burgundy which I retrieved from the wine cellar yesterday and put here on the shelf for tonight's dinner?" Beanstock now asked.

Phillis began to shriek again and sobbed into the handkerchief.

"So now I'm also a drunkard!"

Beanstock pushed the small group out of the cold storage room.

"When did you put the pasty on the shelf?" he asked the cook.

"This morning at around 10:00, just after I had finished making it. Oh, what a triumph it was", the cook enthused, "with juicy lamb and a topping of puff pastry that melts in your mouth."

The butler looked around the kitchen. Two boxes had been placed in the middle of the counter among the collection of pots and bowls. One box was filled with assorted vegetables, whereas the other was empty.

"What are those boxes for?" he asked.

This time Phillis answered, still sobbing.

"Farmer Pitsch's son brought them this morning. The chickens for Friday's dinner were in the empty box, I put them in the pantry."

"Where were you at that time, Mrs Porkpie?" the butler wanted to know. He was in his element. At last he had the plum opportunity to solve a case, just like the protagonist in one of his mystery novels.

"I was with Mrs Argyle after I pointed out we urgently needed some more flour. She started to lecture me and told me I ought to have told her a week ago and there should still be plenty left. Finally, I convinced her to check for herself whether there was enough flour. The whole situation was very unpleasant. Anyway, she eventually made a note of it and then went up to see Bernice to finish getting things ready."

The butler glanced at Mrs Porkpie chastisingly.

"And what about you, Phillis? Were you here the whole time?"

Phillis looked down to the floor and blushed.

"I went to the garage for a moment."

The cook looked at the girl in surprise. "What were you doing there, young lady?" she asked.

"I brought Gonzales a cup of tea. He was very busy and asked me for some this morning. What's the big deal, anyway?"

Beanstock cleared his throat.

He knew perfectly well that the ladies in this house were fascinated by the fiery Gonzales and that they availed themselves of any opportunity to flirt with him.

"What time was this, Phillis?" the butler asked.

"Well, I don't know. Sammy Pitsch had just left."

"What type of shoes was Sammy Pitsch wearing today?"

All those present looked at the butler blankly. No one understood this question and they visibly strained to remember. Meanwhile, Mortecai had wriggled out of the gardener's arm, then slowly and quietly sneaked past the group towards the storage room. Beanstock, however, caught the cat and pushed him out the back door.

"Well, I think Sammy was wearing rubber boots",

Phillis piped up.

"That's what I thought", the butler announced. "Now get back to work."

"But where are these items now?"

Mr Herringbone asked. "Tell me, Mr Beanstock. You surely don't believe that little Sammy has anything to do with the disappearing objects, do you?"

Beanstock waved his hand and everyone scuttled back to their respective tasks. He headed for Sir Percival's house. After knocking and entering, he approached his employer and explained the entire dreadful story. Sir Percival was certain that it had not been Sammy Pitsch. Everyone was quite fond of the 17-year-old boy whom everybody described as very efficient and responsible.

"Oh, Beanstock, it can't be him. Perhaps there's a very simple explanation. Mrs Porkpie put the pasty elsewhere, the bottle of wine is still in the cellar, the rose died and, well, we needn't make mention of my wife's fountain pen. She's already lost it countless times, and it always ended up being her own fault."

"Yes, Sir, I frankly agree with you regarding the fountain pen, and I will start searching for it straightaway. But the traces in the cold storage room undoubtedly originate from rubber boots and the timeline also fits. I suspect Sammy overheard Phillis going into the garage with a cup of tea and returned to the house. Don't these missing objects remind you of anything, Sir?!"

The visibly perplexed lord of the manor looked at Beanstock questioningly.

"These are precisely the items required for a picnic with a young lady, don't you think, Sir? And if you wanted to keep this rendezvous a secret from your parents, you'd have to look for the necessary accoutrements elsewhere."

Sir Percival looked doleful.

Then he yelled, "No, Sammy is a good boy and I don't want anything to happen to him because of some adolescent flight of fancy. Beanstock, you mustn't say anything to anyone, and when Gonzales takes me to the church meeting after lunch you'll join us and go to the farm. Come up with an excuse and try to talk to Sammy alone. He will surely own up to his foolishness. Not to mention, filching a pasty is not grounds for punishment, no matter how delicious it is. And the roses will grow back again."

The butler replied with a slight smile, "I had hoped you'd arrive at this decision. I'm going to look for the pen now, I already have an idea where I might find it. Lady Fedora went to the herb garden immediately after breakfast today, she wanted to check on the dill blossoms."

"Beanstock, you have what it takes to be a great detective. I am proud of you."

The butler left the house through the front entrance. He passed the large ginkgo tree, where the path led him behind the house and into the enclosed herb garden.

The garden was rife with the scent of its lush bushes of camomile, sage, parsley and dill. Ceramic pots filled with basil and thyme were situated next to the dill as they awaited a place to be planted by the gardener. Beanstock took a closer look at the pots. All of a sudden, a meddlesome sunray shone its light on a shiny surface which cast a glint back into Beanstock's eyes. It was the fountain pen, lodged in one of the thyme pots, as though Lady Fedora had attempted to grow a crop of fountain pens. Beanstock retrieved it from the pot and cleaned it.

This golden fountain pen had been through a lot in its life. On several occasions, all the servants had lain on the floors of the house in a valiant search for the treasured pen under the cupboards and chests of drawers.

They had even once found it in Milady's pinned-up hair. Since she had been holding the cap in her hand, some of the blue ink had ended up there and she had walked around with blue streaks for days.

He was now able to return the little maverick to the hands of its very delighted owner, and thus Lady Fedora's career was saved once again.

At precisely 2:00 p.m., Gonzales drove the freshly polished grey Bentley in front of the main entrance. Beanstock opened the rear door and Sir Percival got in, sporting his hat, cane and a displeased facial expression. The butler quietly closed the car door and took the front seat next to Gonzales, who looked at him enquiringly.

"Mr. Gonzalez, once we've dropped Sir Percival off, take me to the Pitsch family's farm. You will have sufficient time to pick up the Baronet again afterwards", Beanstock explained. Gonzales gave an acquiescent nod as he started the engine.

They soon reached the old church, whose architecture consisted of a strange mixture of styles: its tower featured solid Romanesque simplicity, while the spire on top was purely a Gothic pointed helmet. The nave had windows with Tudor glazing and multicolour glass, while the side aisles also had wide Romanesque windows without any particular adornment. The front entrance portal could almost be described as an attempt to incorporate Italian Baroque into an English building. The interior comprised a combination of even more architectural styles. One corner of the crypt appeared as though a pagan wishing tree had been set in one of the stone reliefs. Father Wilson, a ruddy-cheeked man with a halo of stubborn white hair that framed his head, once claimed that someone had tried to overcrowd all of the various visions of this world into this little church. The good soul of a priest could often be seen sitting in one of the pews, investigating a new discovery in the church from his thick architecture book. But the corpulent man loved his patchwork church, and his eyes would start to sparkle whenever he spoke about it.

After Sir Percival had disappeared in the rectory next to the church, Gonzales continued his drive and stopped at farmer Pitsch's homestead after just a few minutes.

The Pitsch family lived there with their three children Sammy, Brontè and Tara and a ragtag menagerie of animals. Chickens, sheep, cows and at least five cats and two dogs required much attention and care. Fortunately, farmer Pitsch had returned from the war in good health and had been able to manage the farm with his son Sammy.

The two daughters, Tara and Brontè, played with brightly coloured shiny tops that clattered across the pavement.

Little five-year-old Tara jumped for joy when she saw the car approaching. But at the moment she recognised Beanstock, her facial expression darkened; she had likely hoped it was Sir Percival who'd come to see her. The two girls sometimes paid him a visit and he would regale them with the regional legends and folklore. Since the Baronets had no children of their own, it was especially fun for them, particularly since Lady Fedora treated the pair to sweet cakes and cocoa on every occasion.

The butler smiled and leaned over to the girl and tousled her reddish curls.

"Where is your brother Sammy, my dears?"

Ten-year-old Brontë pulled a face at the question, which immediately caught his notice.

"What do you want with him, Sir?" she asked quietly, pushing little Tara aside. Thanks to his fine instincts, Beanstock immediately suspected Brontë must know something of his whereabouts.

"Everything is alright, little girl, I just want to talk to him again about tomorrow's order. So tell me, where is he?"

"He rode his bike to the convent..." Tara could not continue, since her big sister gave her a punch to silence her, which garnered a nasty look from herwhile she rubbed the sore spot.

"We don't know exactly where he wanted to go. But he might still be taking some things to the *Rosebud* Hotel", Brontë tried to mediate.

The butler smiled, bade farewell and got into the car. In the rear view mirror he could see the two girls arguing and a knowing smile appeared on his face.

"We need to go to the old convent ruins, Gonzales, there's still enough time."

The chauffeur complied with the butler's wishes and crossed Parsley Field, kept to the right of the River Shirty and eventually stopped at some distance from the picturesque ruins.

"Wait here, please, I'll be back very soon", Beanstock advised.

He walked through the stone portal of the convent.

It was the only vestige of the Romanesque monastery building, save for a few crumbling walls and the stone altar. Trees and flowering shrubs had taken root and created a romantic ambience that was very popular with the village youth. A bicycle leaned against the side of the altar. It was quiet, except for a lone blackbird loudly proclaiming its joie de vivre. Dragonflies buzzed through the meadow of which some areas were trampled. Beanstock walked around the stone altar and finally found Sammy Pitsch huddling there.

The lanky boy with the curly blond hair and freckled face did not move. The missing objects from Parsley Manor were resting on a blanket beside him.

"Leave me alone. I'll pay for the things, unless you're going to call the constable right away", the boy murmured, his teeth clenched.

Beanstock could see tears coursing down Sammy's face. He sat down slowly and gingerly next to him.

"Nobody is going to call the police, my boy. Sir Percival is only interested in why you did it. Who were you trying to impress?"

Sammy looked up and for the second time that day Beanstock offered a white handkerchief to wipe away tears.

"I wanted to invite someone special to a picnic. But she didn't show up. Instead, she laughed at me when I went to pick her up."

47

"Can you tell me the name of your object of affection if I promise my absolute silence?"

Sammy sniffled again. "Miss Summerset. I love her."

Only a seventeen-year-old boy could voice this heartfelt sentiment with such conviction. He looked at the butler expectantly.

It was plain to see that Sammy feared being laughed at again.

But he had completely misjudged Beanstock.

The butler solemnly put his arm around the boy's shoulders, looked at him reassuringly and said, "My dear young friend, you have certainly set your standards high for your first love affair, haven't you? I know the rejection will hurt for a while, but I promise you that you will overcome it soon enough. This peccadillo will be forgotten before you know it, latest by the time you meet a nice girl your own age.

Besides, she would be far too old for you, don't you think? Nevertheless: you have my utmost respect, my boy. I don't think I would have dared to ask such a fine lady out on a date at your age."

Sammy's tears had dried in the meantime and he could manage a slight smile again. "What are we going to do now, Mr Beanstock?"

"It's quite a simple matter. I'll take the wine, the roses and the pasty, while you take the blanket and your bicycle and go home. I'm sure your sisters are waiting for their big brother. So, how do you feel about my idea? Once we're finished we can forget the whole matter."

Sammy nodded gratefully and the two stood up. The teenager took his bike and rode off. He then stopped briefly, turned to the butler and said, "Thank you, Mr Beanstock, that's mighty kind of you."

Then he disappeared behind the trees.

When the butler returned to the car with his reclaimed treasures, Gonzales could scarcely conceal his amazement. He hadn't seen Sammy and thus could not fathom where these objects had come from. And Beanstock would not divulge any information to this end.

After collecting their employer from the unwelcome meeting, they returned home. Beanstock briefly informed Sir Percival of the details in the library. Sir Percival was very pleased with his butler's work and benignly smiled at the whimsical and daring advances of young Sammy Pitsch.

"Yes, you may not be aware of this, Beanstock", he proclaimed vaingloriously, "but I was quite the Don Juan back in my youth. Many a bucolic beauty fell in love with my beautiful eyes."

He enthusiastically glanced at the ceiling on which numerous cute little cherubs had been painted who seemed to peer down at the portly, ruddy-cheeked baronet.

"There's no doubt about it, Sir", Beanstock replied loyally.

Equipped with this newfound vitality, his employer whistled to summon Junior, opened the door to the back terrace and set off on his daily afternoon walk, cheerfully whistling all the while. As always, Junior was overjoyed at this daily activity and romped around his master in frenzied leaps and bounds.

Mortecai, the grey tomcat, was about to start his scavenging expedition, but changed his mind upon seeing Junior. The two animals were not the best of friends; torn scraps of fur and bloody scratches on both creatures were a testimony to their enmity.

Mrs Porkpie returned her pasty creation to the freezer with a contented smile, whereas Mr Herringbone picked up the prize-winning rose while the bottle of exquisite Burgundy was placed on the shelf until dinner.

Everything was in shipshape order again and Beanstock was overwhelmed with joy to have solved a case. Not to mention, the case had been duly settled without a victim or perpetrator. What more could he possibly ask for? No one asked any more questions or was inquisitive about how or why the items had disappeared. All the servants knew about the butler's discretion and to this end no further questions were raised.

Sir Percival recounted the incident only to his wife that evening while ensconced in his soft duvet. As was her evening custom, Lady Fedora sat beside him in their oversized bed with its turned columns and antique pink damask curtains. Round spectacles were perched on her nose as she read one of those romance novels that were in vogue.

"Well, I believe our good Beanstock is a romantic deep down in his butler's heart. Poor Sammy. We shan't remind him ever again. You two have done well. Oh, young people these days..." Heaving a heavy sigh, she again devoted her attention to her novel.

"My dear Fedora, you can truly still be considered as youthful, if I may say so", Sir Percival sweet-talked his wife.

She smiled.

"You've always been such a hopeless romantic, Perci!"

Parsley Manor slowly wound down for the night. In the kitchen, Phillis was busy putting the last of the clean knives back in the drawer. She yawned.

Mrs Porkpie stored her famous sponge cake in the pantry. Tomorrow, it would turn into a veritable work of art with the addition of raspberry jelly and buttercream. She sent Phillis to bed. The next few days would surely be busy: details for dinner preparations on Friday and the reception on Saturday were to be carried out. She switched off the light in the kitchen and went upstairs to her room.

By this time, servant Harrison had already been soundly snoring for an hour. Bernice and Filomena the maid chatted audibly and giggled as they went upstairs. Mr Beanstock looked up from his mystery novel in his room and shook his head at their display of hijinks.

It was Gonzales's night off, and in all likelihood he would spend it at O'Donoghue's pub, where he had made friends with the landlord. Gonzales was forced to leave Spain long before the war. But he kept tight-lipped about that part of his life.

The gardener checked his Moonlight Shadow rose one last time to ensure that indeed nothing had happened to it.

Mortecai watched him with half-closed eyes and seemed to wonder when he would finally take care of his cat instead of this foul-smelling green matter.

In the housekeeper's office, the light remained switched on until the next morning. The letter she had received in the post today truly unsettled her. She had taken a stack of yellowed letters bound together with a faded green ribbon out of her locked box. Her expression increasingly darkened as she went through them one by one.

Meanwhile, Parsley Manor was fast asleep, without any inkling that something evil was afoot.

Parsley Field

Mr Partridge began each working day of his beloved vocation in the postal service with the Baronets of Parsley. After crossing the River Shirty, he alit from his bike and briefly reviewed the contents of his bag. He had taken out two letters and now entered the venerable pub of Parsley Field village, where the small-town postman usually started his tour. It was a pleasant opportunity to enjoy an early ale or, in case he got delayed, a late porter.

It was still early in the morning and the landlord, Sean O'Donoghue, was sitting at one of his brightly polished tables while reading the paper and drinking his morning tea. He was a tall, muscular man in his forties. His curly dark brown hair fell to his shoulders, and he rather resembled a swashbuckling buccaneer with his bright blue eyes. Many years ago, his parents had moved from Ireland to Parsley Field and opened the pub in the old, nearly dilapidated Parsley Inn that same year. Sean's father had quickly made a name for himself by virtue of his excellent beers and whiskies, but was infamous for his countless hair-raising, outlandish stories from his Irish days. The pub soon became a major attraction in the county.

Sean now ran the pub under the new name, *Jack O'Lantern*. The establishment had the lingering aroma of tobacco, old wood and good whisky.

"A letter from the *mansion* for you, Sean. Guess they must've forced themselves to send an invitation. Seems they're expecting a visitor on Friday. At least that's what my little girl told me yesterday, though she didn't exactly know any names."

The postman curiously looked at the fine letter written on handmade paper. Sean took it, cast it aside without so much as a glance and delved back into his newspaper, grumbling all the while. Mr Partridge continued expectantly watching him for a while. The landlord seemed to have no intention of picking up the tab for an early ale today. He sighed deeply and audibly, which didn't seem to faze O'Donoghue in the least. Mr Partridge shrugged his shoulders and made his way out.

Sean watched him go, smiling and shaking his head.

His next stop was the widow Bloom's country shop next door, which was quite popular in the area. It was a very pretty shop, stocked with a large variety of colourful, eye-catching goods against a backdrop of two large white lattice windows to the left and right of the entrance. Buckets filled with white and blue hydrangeas had been placed in front of the showcase of wares. A white wooden bench invited customers to relax.

Within two steps upon entering the shop, one would encounter the widow Bloom – a white-haired lady who always had a smile – behind a dark wooden counter with elaborate carvings along its sides. Her husband, Colonel Bloom, had been killed in the war, thus she now ran this shop by herself. The range of products served to improve life in the countryside, ranging from cosmetics for the lady to rubber boots for the gentleman, and even fine Chinese porcelain. Any locally unattainable merchandise was ordered from nearby London. She enjoyed her reputation of being able to procure just about anything. Most of the time, she could be seen brooding over her books early in the morning, round gold-rimmed glasses perched on her nose, and running her finger down the columns of sales figures.

As soon as she saw the postman, she greeted him at the door.

"Anything today, Mr Partridge? I've been expecting a parcel for a very long time indeed, as you know."

"I'm sorry, Mrs Bloom, no parcel for you. But there *is* a letter from the *mansion*."

He handed her the thick letter of handmade paper with its fine penmanship and curiously followed her into the shop. But the widow Bloom did not accord him the favour he had hoped for. She turned the letter back and forth and finally put it in one of the drawers.

"Anything else, Mr Partridge? Do you need tobacco or something?" she asked the postman when she saw him waiting expectantly in the doorway. Then she smiled knowingly and held out the round, thick jar of raspberry sweets he was partial to. Mr Partridge sighed, reached into the jar, put the candy into his mouth and smacked it with pleasure.

"No, thanks, I'm fine", he replied disappointedly.

While outside standing by his bike, he looked at the address for the next letter and his expression brightened. He started to grin and hastened his way to the pharmacy across the large square past the old thick oak tree in its centre.

The pharmacy was the only place to get medicine in this area; residents had to travel here from many other towns. Parsley Field had been fortunate when the old pharmacist James Hoppleton initially established himself here.

But now his son George was running the pharmacy. Since he had two children – a son and a daughter – the tradition was expected to continue.

The building was painted bright green and had two large lattice windows to the left and right of the entrance, exactly like the widow Bloom's shop. As opposed to the tubs of hydrangeas at Mrs Bloom's store, bright red geraniums had been placed in front of the windows. However, there was also a painted green bench on the premises.

It was common knowledge in the village that the widow Bloom and the pharmacist's wife were bitter adversaries. Every year the two of them engaged in a ludicrous competition for the most beautiful shop.

When the postman opened the door and the familiar ringing sounded above him, the two ladies of the family were already standing in front of him, looking at him expectantly. Hoppleton's daughter Pamela, a pretty girl with long blonde hair, snatched the handmade paper envelope right out of his hand.

"Could this be what I think it is? Tell me, Partridge, is it what it's supposed to be, and is it what I want it to be?"

"Um, what yes, no, yes, um, what was your question again?" the overwhelmed postman stammered.

"Let the man finish, Pam, you're getting carried away. Mind your manners, my child, mind your manners!" Mrs Hoppleton wrested the envelope from her daughter's hand and opened it excruciatingly slowly.

At last, the postman thought, *I knew this would work out in my favour here.*

Mrs Hoppleton pulled out the sheet of paper with the coat of arms at its top centre and unfolded it.

"Mother, unless you tell me what it says immediately, I'm going to faint", Pamela announced.

Annoyed, the pharmacist rested his head in his hands behind the dark wood panelled counter of the pharmacy.

Mrs Hoppleton dropped the paper and shrieked at her daughter: "We've been invited to the reception! Oh my God, what on earth shall we wear?"

They held hands and stared at each other, squealing in delight and disbelief. Their revelry thus granted the postman enough time to pick up the fallen paper and take a quick glance at it.

On the coveted invitation, Lady Fedora had written the following in her exceedingly fine penmanship:

We hereby cordially invite you and your family.
On the occasion of our godchild's visit,
Miss Priscilla Hillman,
we are holding a small reception at Parsley
Manor.

We expect you at 12:00 p.m.
Lady Fedora Parsley and Sir Percival Parsley.

In the interim, the two ladies had disappeared through one of the doors. But their animated chatter was still audible long after.

Meanwhile, the postman's face had taken on a slight pallor. He was glued to the piece of paper in his hand.

"Couldn't you have thrown that confounded letter into the River Shirty? I can't understand what she's playing at, anyway. Why must Lady Fedora invite everyone and their dog to her home? Why can't she display the same condescension like the others of her rank and only invite people of her own station? Then I would be spared the whole disaster with these crazy women. I could only meet the doctor and the vicar once a week in the pub and everything would be in apple-pie order", the pharmacist moaned.

The postman simply shrugged his shoulders, put the letter on the counter, set off for his next customer and pedalled determinedly toward the large thatched house at the end of the village.

This house was where Doctor Winterbottom had established his office and, for reasons of convenience, his sister Rachel Winterbottom likewise had her veterinarian practice. Unless they mixed up their offices, their patients remained content. But on occasion in their joint waiting room, clergyman Wilson – who was suffering from stomach pains – would end up sitting next to the widow Bloom with her cat Peter who was likewise tormented by stomach pains after he had once again discovered and plundered the bag of raspberry sweets.

Both doctors received their invitations. Dr Rachel Winterbottom, a very svelte, pretty woman with a short, ash blonde hairstyle, had a coughing fit while reading the letter.

She handed it to her brother and quickly made her way to her consulting room. Dr Timothy Winterbottom, still the most eligible bachelor in town, read it and raised an eyebrow in disgust. Then he nodded comprehendingly at his sister.

The postman turned his bicycle around and rode back. There was still one invitation to deliver. Mr Partridge had deliberately saved this one for last.

On his way to a hotel where his wife worked at the front desk, the postman passed the railway station, the patchwork church, the chemist's shop, the country shop and pub and pedalled along the River Shirty, across the little wood and finally past the old ruins of the convent destroyed by the Normans so long ago.

The hotel was a beautiful, snow-white Art Deco building with stuccoed high ceilings and colourful leaded doors inside it. The hotel's strange name, *Rosebud,* had belonged to a well-known painter in the 1920s who had also arranged exhibitions in the establishment. According to Parsley Field gossip, he also threw extravagant parties. Even a member of the royal family was rumoured to have been a frequent visitor.

After the painter had passed away at an early age due to his excessive lifestyle, his widow eventually had to sell the house. A wealthy Indian from the former crown colony acquired it, leased some land from Baronet Parsley, established a huge golf course and transformed the premises into a forty-room hotel.

Mr Partridge parked his bike at the side entrance and entered the hotel through the kitchen. Amid the bustling activity, the cook was loudly giving instructions in all directions. The postman nodded to him in acknowledgement and walked through the swinging door into the adjoining hallway where he kept to the right while walking down the long corridor.

He knocked on a large white door and entered after he heard a brief, "Come in." In the small antechamber, Miss Summerset, the secretary, sat at her typewriter, pounding on the keys. She was a beautiful woman with pinned-up long blonde hair and lusciously red-painted lips. She wore a tight burgundy suit and matching high heels. As usual, the postman's ears turned red in her presence. He cleared his throat and held out the mail to her. Smiling, Miss Summerset rose and grabbed the letters, looking coquettishly at him all the while.

"Is that all for today, Mr Partridge?" She whispered into his face with half-closed eyes. Her long, made-up black lashes fluttered. The postman's ears reddened even more

"That's all", he managed to croak out, before he quickly turned around and left.

Miss Summerset knocked on the door to her employer's office and entered.

Gold-framed photographs depicting lush Indian landscapes and palaces hung on the dark red walls of the spacious office. A huge desk bedecked with dark carvings and gold fittings had been placed in front of the large window. The armchair behind this desk was so expansive that it could have been fit for a king.

A tall man standing at the window framed by floral-patterned red curtains was gazing into the garden. White strands were visible in his medium-length black hair. Contrary to the Indian tradition of his wealthy family, he wore a single-breasted tailored suit in dark grey, a gold-interwoven grey tie and dark grey lace-up shoes which were bench made by one of England's finest shoemakers. When Miss Summerset entered, he turned and looked at her questioningly.

"I informed you I didn't want to be disturbed", he said in a soft, quiet voice.

"I'm very sorry, Mr Divari, but this cannot wait. It's a letter from the *mansion*."

Parsley Manor was universally known as the *mansion*. Everyone understood what it meant. The Indian raised an eyebrow and took the letter. Miss Summerset gave him a curt nod and returned to her office.

Davinder Divari opened the envelope with a pointy gold letter opener, took out the heavy sheet of handmade paper and unfolded it slowly, as though he dreaded the prospect of bad news. After reading it several times, he pressed a button on his desk. Miss Summerset appeared with pad and pencil in hand. He handed her the invitation.

"Please convey my acknowledgement of the invitation and my regret at not being able to attend. With kind regards and so on and so forth... you know the routine. Then send it to Parsley Manor today."

The secretary looked at him sympathetically after a quick glance at the letter.

"But Mr Divari, this is a very important invitation. The hotel must maintain its favourable connections with the Baronets. You know how often Sir Percival and his wife have recommended the *Rosebud*. Besides, you wanted to participate more frequently in the county's social life. This reception would be an ideal opportunity. I'm sure all the influential people from Parsley Field will be there. Not to mention the Hollywood diva: what an ideal opportunity to establish connections across the pond."

The Indian sighed.

"You are right, as usual. I should try to be a bit more accommodating. Alright, confirm my attendance. And you shall accompany me."

Miss Summerset forced a smile and returned to her work. Back at her desk, she glanced at the invitation with pursed lips. She looked through the window into a distant time that nobody else was privy to. Then she took a deep breath and continued pounding at the keys.

Meanwhile the postman had gone down the hall to the front desk where his wife was busy sorting through the recent registrations behind the counter. When she looked up and noticed her husband approaching, her brow visibly furrowed in anger.

"Darling, your ears are red again. You needn't say a thing. I know where you've been." Angrily, she turned her attention back to the registrations.

Mr Partridge sidestepped past the counter and disappeared quickly through the main entrance. He had actually hoped for a decent cup of tea and a tea cake. Now he had to content himself with a cup of tea in the pub, where there were no sumptuous scones at that hour. Under the circumstances, he could get by with an early whisky. He drew a deep, sad breath, mounted his bike and rode slowly back to Parsley Field. His mind was racing.

Shouldn't he have told his wife who was expected at the *mansion*?

A Diva Arrives

A strange gathering of people could be seen at Parsley Field Station that day. Groups of young girls and boys were scattered along the platform, which made stationmaster Mr Templar terribly ill at ease.

Mr Templar sat on his bench in front of the old station while sipping his sweet tea, observing a crowd to which he was not accustomed. He was especially surprised that so many young people from the neighbouring village had come all the way here. After all, the neighbouring village had a platform of its own. Not as nice as the one in Parsley Field, mind you, Mr Templar thought and allowed himself a satisfied smile.

He repeatedly looked at the big old clock encased in wrought-iron filigree which jutted out onto the platform.

As a rule, there were not many passengers on the small platform on Friday evenings. Furthermore, it was not a time when many residents wanted to travel. He did not know what to make of it.

Ten minutes before the arrival of the evening train

from London, the chauffeur of Parsley Manor drove up to the station. Mr Templar was now completely convinced he must have forgotten something. He grew increasingly nervous as he put his half-full cup of tea on the station window and made his way to the platform.

Gonzales got out of the pristinely polished Bentley. He had put on his best uniform, the one with shiny gold buttons, and the hat Sir Percival had bought him in London. He only wore it on very special occasions and was quite vigilant about keeping it in immaculate condition. He gave the excited stationmaster a slight nod and looked at the many people in amazement. The train arrived on time at exactly 6:20 p.m.

Mr Templar tried to disperse the curiously approaching people from the edge of the platform. The train stopped with a screeching sound. At the same moment, both the conductor and his stoker stuck their heads out of the window of the locomotive, anxiously glancing behind them.

Mr Templar approached the men and asked about the reason for all the commotion.

"Is that Winston Churchill on the train, by any chance?"

The stoker, a lanky man with thinning hair beneath his dirty cap, grinned and lit a cigarette.

"Well, you should know by now. A highfalutin visitor from Hollywood is in town. Take a good look at this beauty, Templar. She's the kind of woman I could really take a shine to."

"And she won't even deem you worth a look, Charly. You'd best turn up the heat now. We're leaving straightaway", the engine driver scolded. At that moment, the boisterous conversations on the platform fell silent and a murmur went through the crowd.

A few of the spectators simply stood there stock-still, their mouths agape. The door of one of the compartments had opened. Gonzales immediately hurried to the steps of the train and reached out his hand to assist the mysterious passenger. At first nothing was to be seen save for a small, delicate foot in an exquisite emerald green shoe with a perilously high heel. And then an otherworldly beauty appeared in the doorway of the train. In order to intensify her impression on her admirers, she made a momentary dramatic pause on the stairs as she gazed around, her lids half-closed.

She wore an emerald green skirt suit that revealed more than it actually concealed. As was befitting of her mysterious aura, she then wrapped her snow-white fur stole around her shoulders with a dramatic flourish before taking another step down the stairs. She proceeded to grab the chauffeur's hand, after which he was at a loss for words for quite possibly the first time in his life.

"*Diablito*", he whispered softly.

Her light blue eyes were scarcely visible under the long black lashes, and her mouth, painted with dark red lipstick, smiled disdainfully.

Inga Hillman was fully aware of the impact on her audience and enjoyed it to the fullest. She shook her short, jet-black bobbed hair in a befittingly Hollywood gesture and stepped onto the platform. Her long, sparkling diamond earrings tinkled softly. A hint of vanilla filled the air.

A din of whispers surged through the crowd.

Old Mrs Pommerton tugged at the stationmaster's sleeve.

"When will the train finally be leaving, Mr Templar? I've got to see my daughter. She's very ill, you know. What's all the fuss about?" she yelled in her distinctive, piercing voice, which could instantly cause a massive earache. Due to her hardness of hearing, she was naturally unaware of its intensity. Mr Templar quickly helped her board the train and closed the door behind her, the old lady complaining all the while. She opened one of the windows with great difficulty and shouted at Mr Templar, "Oh dear, the basket full of chicken broth for my daughter is still outside!"

The stationmaster quickly grabbed the basket and handed it to her through the compartment window.

Gonzales accompanied Miss Hillman to the car and stowed her luggage which consisted of no fewer than four suitcases, one bag, and two hat boxes. By happenstance, Mr Van Horten had telephoned that afternoon to inform he would be late and would likely travel in his own vehicle. Gonzales wheezed in exhaustion after having loaded the onerous luggage.

Mr Templar raised his signalling wand and was more than happy when the train – as well as the unwelcome hordes – eventually left the station. He reached into his trouser pocket, pulled out a large handkerchief and wiped the beads of sweat from his forehead.

In the meantime, some of the young people were already swarming around the Bentley, trying to catch another glimpse of the Hollywood starlet. Inga raised her left arm and began to wave like Queen Elizabeth, although the car was still stationary. She smiled weakly and forbearingly.

The car eventually started to move and cautiously made its way through the crowd of people in the street towards the River Shirty.

Inga Hillman retrieved a small box from her shiny silver bag and powdered her nose. Gonzales watched her surreptitiously from the rear-view mirror – or so he thought. After she had finished, she winked at him, ensconced herself in her fur stole and closed her eyes.

The chauffeur would have been well pleased for the drive to take a little longer, but Parsley Manor was not very far away from the village, and within a few minutes he turned onto the long driveway to the mansion and stopped next to the ginkgo tree. The front door burst open immediately and Lady Fedora excitedly tore out of the house, flung the car door open and embraced her godchild exuberantly.

"My dear Priscilla, when did we last meet? It's been far too long", Milady exclaimed.

The young woman stepped out of the car, adjusted her fur stole, peered at the façade of the venerable house, and whispered affectedly, "Yes, it's been such a long, very long time, dear Fedora. But please call me Inga. I see that nothing around here has changed."

Lady Fedora was slightly taken aback at the uncharitable remark, but kept a stiff upper lip, linked arms with the godchild she had missed for so long and ushered her into the house. In the meantime, the servants had also shown up in freshly starched aprons and shirts, ready to offer their services to their prominent guest. Lady Fedora briefly introduced the servants and informed Inga that her maid Filomena was to be exclusively at her disposal during her visit to Parsley Manor.

Miss Hillman seemed utterly indifferent.

"Dear Fedora, I am a bit exhausted. I would like to be shown my room and have a short rest." She retrieved a cigarette from a gold case, placed it in a long golden cigarette holder and looked beseechingly for assistance. Mr Beanstock took a lighter from his pocket and held the flame towards the cigarette. He bowed his head and stepped back into the line of servants.

Lady Fedora briefly cleared her throat.

"Of course, my dear. Filomena will show you the green room. We hope it will meet your expectations. Dinner is served at 8:00 p.m.; we hope our second guest will also have arrived by then."

Filomena and the servant Harrison took the luggage and made their way upstairs to the guest rooms, while the other servants returned to work as quickly as possible. They had a lot of details to discuss. It was only the butler who remained in his place, discreetly fixing his gaze at the floor. Lady Fedora felt like she had just encountered a stranger.

"I would like you to inconspicuously distribute some ashtrays around the house, Beanstock. I didn't realise she's a smoker. This is as new to me as the name Inga", Lady Fedora uttered in a low voice. At that moment, Sir Percival arrived with a clangour, Junior in tow after their long walk. He immediately realised his wife was distraught.

"Everything okay, Darling? Sorry I'm a bit late", he said tentatively. "Where is our honoured guest? Has she arrived yet?" He surveyed the room before he inquiringly glanced at the butler.

"Miss Hillman arrived on time and will take a short repose until dinner, Sir. Would you mind if I continued to oversee the preparations?"

Sir Percival nodded approvingly.

"Beanstock, kindly bring a decent cup of tea to the

salon", the master of the house requested, without taking his eyes off his wife.

"With your permission, I will also bring the whisky decanter into the salon, Sir", the butler replied sympathetically.

"What would we do without you?" Lady Fedora asked, and the butler noticed a small tear glistening in one of her eyes.

"Whatever happened to all the blonde curls, the cute freckles, and the adorable pink socks?" she murmured on her way to the salon. Sir Percival smiled benevolently and winked, signalling Beanstock to hurry with the whisky.

"Everything is okay, Darling, calm down", Sir Percival whispered to his wife and gently guided her into the salon. "She was such a sweet child and so funny. Her parents were very proud of her. Oh, why did they have to die so soon...?" Lady Fedora was beside herself.

A few minutes before 8:00 p.m., the expected sound of tyres crunching on the gravel path in front of the house was finally heard.

The bell rang and Beanstock leisurely approached the door, as was typical of him. A black Bugatti Atalante sat parked in front of the house.

Gonzales quickly left the garage where he was still working on his own car at such a late hour, an old Ford he had discovered in his friend O'Donoghue's garage. The landlord of the local pub had bequeathed it to him with the words "It's beyond repair." Gonzales was loathe to accept this ominous verdict and spent every spare moment trying to revive the old car.

He walked around the car of the newly arrived guest like a panther ready to leap at its prey. Beanstock frowned when he witnessed the scene unfolding in front of him.

A tall, svelte gentleman stood in front of the car and observed the chauffeur – who seemed completely preoccupied – with obvious amusement. Silver-grey hair peeked out from under his brown felt hat, and his exquisitely tailored dark brown suit fit like a glove. Everything about the gentleman was deliberately well-coordinated.

Only his cold, implacable eyes contradicted his sophisticated appearance. The butler was always wise to such inconsistencies within mere seconds. He could usually judge people very quickly and was rarely wrong. To his mind, this gentleman was a cold and calculating egoist who never allowed himself to reveal any emotions or vulnerability.

Mr Van Horten, Lady Fedora's publisher from London, was a 55-year-old bachelor who had rightfully earned the distinction of being one of the most affluent individuals in his profession.

"This beauty is a Bugatti Type 57 S Atalante", Gonzales whispered reverently, "only very few of them were ever produced."

Mr Van Horten opened the boot and retrieved a small crocodile leather suitcase, as well as a black briefcase and a garment bag. Mr Beanstock disencumbered him of his luggage.

"Allow me to welcome you to Parsley Manor, Sir."

The hosts appeared from the salon. Lady Fedora had changed her clothes and was now elegantly clad in a long dark green dress adorned with a beautiful emerald brooch.

A papillote was visible in her hair. Beanstock knew that this utensil did not belong there at that moment. *Filomena Arbuckle! I must immediately have a word with Milady's maid again*, he thought to himself and inconspicuously removed the wooden object from Lady Fedora's hair. The lady's maid was known for her lack of attention to detail; Beanstock had already made her aware of such issues several times. Although Miss Arbuckle had acknowledged them as such, she never attempted to correct her slipshod ways.

Sir Percival wore his dark blue dinner suit and welcomed the new guest in his customarily flagrant manner. Junior jumped around the small group as if high-strung and had to be admonished. Harrison, very neatly dressed in a suit, took the suitcase and the garment bag from the butler, and carried the items upstairs to the blue guest room; the publisher would not allow anyone else to touch his briefcase.

Beanstock took the guest's hat and the small party repaired to the salon for an aperitif before dinner. The butler mixed all the beverages with his customary proficiency.

Mr Van Horten did not waste any time cutting to the chase. "My dear Lady Fedora, many thanks for your invitation, it is urgent that we discuss your forthcoming book *The Herbs in My Garden*. There are a few discrepancies that ought to be settled."

Lady Fedora looked at him questioningly. "What discrepancies? You haven't told me anything of the sort."

"But surely not tonight, especially on such a beautiful evening", Sir Percival intervened, raising his glass of gin and tonic. Mr Van Horten smiled agreeably. The master of the house was evidently in his element.

"Did you know that even the ancient Romans appreciated and exploited the benefits of a certain aperitif? The citizens of Rome were aware of the appetising effect of herbs dissolved in wine, and learned it could also alleviate stomach troubles. Which meant the Romans could look forward to a sumptuous feast *and* a Roman orgy without the risk of any nasty repercussions." He guffawed loudly at his off-colour joke.

"Oh, have I just heard we've been invited to a Roman orgy? In that case I am afraid I'm not properly dressed." Miss Hillman was playing it up to her audience, as usual.

She posed theatrically in the doorway to the salon with a sensual smile on her red lips. She wore a long, flowing white silk dress embroidered with a multitude of gold sequins and her pumps were interwoven with gold. Glittery elbow-length gloves completed her movie star ensemble.

Sir Percival choked on the last word which induced a coughing fit and had to quickly take a sip of his drink when he noticed his wife's mortified facial expression. Lady Fedora stepped in for him and introduced the guests to each other, "May I introduce Mr Van Horten, Miss Inga Hillman, my godchild."

Beanstock, who was mixing a martini for Miss Hillman, realised that the publisher had stopped short for a moment at the sight of the celebrity. A shadow of recognition crossed his face, prompting sweat beads to appear on his forehead. Beanstock ascribed it to the actress's exciting performance – which would make an indelible impression on every man.

Miss Hillman daintily offered her right hand to Mr Van Horten and he bowed briefly.

An uncomfortable silence filled the room.

One could have heard a pin drop. Inga Hillman gave the publisher an oddly appraising look. "Haven't we met before, Mr Van Horten?" she asked him.

Sir Percival took a breath and was about to change the subject, but his wife's sidelong glance unambiguously signalled him to refrain. Fortunately, the dinner gong sounded at that moment and thus interrupted the awkward situation. They proceeded to the dining room.

Bernice and Phillis had set the table with white damask cloth, white tableware bearing the Baronets' coat of arms, and the estate's best silverware. The gardener had placed a beautiful rose arrangement at the centre of the table. The impeccable table setting once again brought a contented smile to Lady Fedora's face.

After the guests had taken their places, the first course, a fine broth, was served. The main course comprised crispy fried chicken with a medley of vegetables, whereupon the cook, Mrs Porkpie, appeared, beaming with pride, and placed her prized pasty creation in front of Miss Hillman's plate. Lady Fedora nodded at her with a wry smile.

The cook proudly explained, "I prepared this pasty especially for you since you always asked for it as a child whenever you stayed with us. Do you remember all the times you and your dolls sat with me in my kitchen?"

Miss Hillman seemed rather nonplussed and simply stared at the pasty, the cook and finally at her hostess. In her affected ethereal voice, she remarked: "Well, perhaps I did, but I haven't eaten that kind of food for years. It's terribly unhealthy, greasy – and far too rich."

Lady Fedora closed her eyes for a split second

duly mortified at Inga's insensitive response.

She knew how much Mrs Porkpie had been looking forward to Priscilla – or Inga or whatever her name was. It would take some time to placate the cook. She nodded to the thoroughly perplexed Mrs Porkpie and Beanstock intimated for her to leave, along with the pasty.

When she appeared in the kitchen with her culinary masterpiece, utterly forlorn and woebegone, everyone in the room immediately realised it had not turned out as expected. The cook fetched forks, set the pasty on the table, and furiously stabbed the cutlery into it. "Go on and eat, but don't you dare say anything about it." No one was brave enough to defy her order.

Gonzales, who had just come in, saw the wonderful pasty – including the constellation of cutlery on the table – grabbed a fork and shovelled a huge fat-drenched morsel into his mouth.

"Oh, Señora Porkpie, how wonderful, *dios mio*, this is splendid. You are a true artist."

The cook blushed and smiled. Everyone in the room, even Mrs Argyle, now quickly helped themselves to her creation and was lavish in their praise.

Meanwhile, the evening in the dining room carried on just as it had begun, with awkward silence and Sir Percival's nervous remarks. His sigh of relief when the last course, an exquisite soufflé, was served inevitably captured his wife's attention – as well as the evil eye.

Miss Hillman excused herself immediately after dinner, complaining of fatigue and a punishing headache, and then retired for the evening. Sir Percival made his sentiments known with another laboured sigh.

His wife, by contrast, lapsed into an embarrassed silence, and was thus disinclined to discuss business with her publisher. She apologised to her guest and postponed their business meeting until the next day. She then paid a brief visit to the kitchen, thanked her staff for their excellent work, and abundantly praised Mrs Porkpie before she repaired to her studio, where the lights remained on till the next morning.

Lady Fedora's publisher sat with the lord of the house in the library's comfortable leather armchairs and enjoyed a superb red Burgundy.

"Where did you make the acquaintance of Miss Hillman, Sir Percival?"

"The Hillman family lived nearby in one of the beautiful old mansions. We've been friends with them for as long as I can remember. So long ago that I even played in the sandbox with Patrik Hillman."

Sir Percival chortled at his joke.

"I was best man at his wedding, and he at mine after I had met my Fedora. And when their children were born, we became godparents. It's a long, tragic story."

"How so?" asked Van Horten. In the interim the butler had entered the room, and again noticed the man's cold, calculating look he had previously observed.

"Well, one day there was a terrible accident which claimed the lives of my friends, whereupon the two daughters were suddenly all alone. An aunt in London took care of them and we lost sight of our godchildren as a result. After such a long time, we've only just met Priscilla again."

"What about her sister?"

The man's a touch too curious, Beanstock thought as he left the room with the empty bottle of Burgundy.

"Oh, that was even more tragic", Sir Percival confided to his counterpart.

"Priscilla was 16 and Emely was 18 at the time. Emely was adversely affected by her parents' death and lapsed into a deep depression. Back then we considered the aunt might be overreacting when she brought the poor girl to a psychiatric hospital in London. My wife still bitterly chastises herself over this. She tried to contact the aunt, she truly wanted to help. But the aunt responded with a nasty letter and unequivocally demanded for Fedora to stop interfering.

I believe that aunt was a terribly cold-hearted woman. When Emely suddenly died in the psychiatric hospital, we were completely shocked.

Priscilla was only 18 years old at the time. We learned the whole tragic story from their former nanny, who was still in contact with their aunt. Priscilla didn't stay with this horrible woman for long and soon eloped. Then she somehow managed to achieve stardom in Hollywood."

Sir Percival thoughtfully raised his glass as he reminisced over the past and shook his head in perplexion. "A story that would make for an incredible novel, don't you agree, Mr Van Horten?"

"You're absolutely right, Sir Percival!" he exclaimed. The publisher had apparently heard enough, stood up, and bade his host a good night.

Once Mr Van Horten had gone to his room, Sir Percival checked in on his wife. She was sitting in her painter's smock at the large drawing table, yet again trying her hand at a dill blossom – alas, to no avail. Her husband recognised it was better to let his wife work in peace in such moments and went to bed, none the wiser she had come in well after midnight. She quietly put on her nightgown and pensively stared at the ceiling for a long while.

Lady Fedora eventually fell asleep, had chaotic dreams which pertained to the past and – as is the case with almost every dream – made very little sense.

The servants of Parsley Manor had also gone to sleep upon completion of their cleaning duties. The housekeeper and the butler were the last of the servants who remained downstairs where they briefly discussed all their respective duties for the next day. They had made it a tradition to check the schedule for the following day on the evening prior to a festivity to ensure no detail was overlooked.

The butler shut his notebook and was about to stand up, satisfied with the discussion at hand, when Mrs Argyle grabbed his arm to hold him back, whereupon he sat down again.

"Is there anything else we need to discuss, Mrs Argyle?" he asked in surprise.

The butler's question seemed to unnerve the housekeeper.

"As you are well aware, I received some interesting mail today", she responded.

The housekeeper audibly gulped, stood up and then took two glasses out of the cupboard. She then momentarily stepped into her office and returned with a small decanter she kept there "for medicinal purposes". After pouring the cherry liqueur, they raised their glasses to each other and enjoyed the cool, smooth aperitif. Despite the pleasant treat, Beanstock felt uneasy.

"You are aware of the adverse circumstances I experienced when I began my employ at Parsley Manor in 1945. Your integrity and empathy helped me immensely in re-establishing myself. Well, I've never told you why I had to leave London at such short notice – and am still reluctant to do so. But this particular letter unsettled me. And I'm at an absolute loss on how to deal with it."

The butler looked at her sympathetically.

"I am only too glad to help you, but unless I know the exact circumstances, it will be very difficult to give you any advice."

The housekeeper took a deep breath.

"What would you do if you knew that there was a dishonest individual in this house; that is, if you discovered that the individual in question is not what he pretends to be? Would you take action or simply turn a blind eye?"

Beanstock contemplated the housekeeper's quandary for a moment. A distinctly pensive wrinkle appeared between his eyebrows.

"Hmmm, does this individual pose any danger to our employers or staff? That would be my first consideration." He looked beseechingly at Mrs Argyle.

She felt uncomfortable and in all likelihood was loath to reveal too much about her source and the information. "I don't believe this individual would directly endanger Parsley Manor and its residents," she responded suggestively.

"In that case I can only give you this advice: Unless you divulge more details about your misgivings, there is little I can do. I would leave the situation as it is and keep an eye on the individual in question. It is hardly our business if that person has something to conceal. We are only obligated to focus our attention on Milady and Sir Percival. All I can ask of you is to remain cautious. But should you discover that our lord and ladyship might come to any harm, act immediately."

The housekeeper nodded in agreement and thanked Beanstock for his support. They emptied their glasses, put them in the sink and went into their respective rooms.

Once the butler was in his chamber, he tried to ascertain whom Mrs Argyle might have implicated. He automatically assumed it was her ladyship's publisher, Mr Van Horten. Something was peculiar about the gentleman and Beanstock decided to keep a keen eye on him.

At that same moment, Mr Van Horten was standing at the window of his appealingly decorated blue room.

He had no regard or appreciation whatsoever for the charming floral-patterned wallpaper embellished with bouquets of forget-me-nots.

The lavender-scented bed linen and the delicate bouquet of roses next to the water carafe likewise completely escaped his attention.

He gazed out of the window, his lips pursed in mischief as he contemplated his situation. He couldn't ascertain whether anyone had recognised him after so much time had passed. It would be best for him to feign an excuse, claim he had urgent work tomorrow after the reception and thus was obligated to return to London. How could he have known that this Miss Hillman character would be at Parsley Manor at the same time? Some cataclysmic coincidence was playing a dirty trick on him. He had immediately noticed the resemblance to her sister, although her outside appearance had considerably changed. But beneath the make-up and the dyed hair, she was still the young girl from his past.

Van Horten forcefully yanked the fine window curtains in frustration. By the time he heard the sound of tearing cloth, it was too late; the curtain now had a long rip as a result of his impetuous actions. He took a small black leather case containing ampoules of clear liquid and some yellowish liquid from his briefcase. He then filled a syringe with the clear liquid and inserted the needle into his vein, feeling considerably better afterwards. He then lay down on the bed, fully clad, and after a few minutes he was fast asleep.

In the opposite green guest room, Inga was sitting at the open window, gazing into the night. Black tears streamed down her face.

The mascara-stained dros ran down onto her shiny silver-white nightgown. She deeply inhaled the smoke from her cigarette. She could not see any light in the distance. Clouds hid the moon and obscured the view of the distant house of her childhood.

Yet it was still there – behind the forest and the

cornfields. It had fallen into disrepair many years ago and had then ultimately been abandoned.

Everything they owned still had to be in that house: her toys, the colourful books and her mother's dressing table from which she had always secretly helped herself. She remembered the halcyon days when she was allowed to go hunting with her father or when her big sister Emely had played Robin Hood with her. How she had loved this hero from Sherwood Forest. The sisters had always argued who would play the hero and who had to be the nasty Sheriff of Nottingham.

It all happened so long ago. And now, of all people, she encountered this vile man here and the myriad terrible memories troubled her again like a bad nightmare. But had he since changed his name? Maybe she was wrong and it wasn't him, after all. Not to mention, she was also no longer the small, insignificant Priscilla Hillman. Now she was the movie star Inga Hillman.

She took a cloth and wiped the tears off her face. As she looked in the mirror, she became harshly aware of the first tell-tale signs of her waning youth: wrinkles around her eyes and mouth. Until now, make-up and rouge had been able to conceal a fair bit of these flaws. But in this new film? She had undergone some tough negotiations. Her, too old for the star role? Ridiculous. The audition and her agent had expertly convinced the studio otherwise. She took out a new cigarette from her golden case and inhaled the smoke.

It was quiet and at that moment the clouds cleared away. There it was. Far away, but one could just barely make it out. Her heartbeat accelerated and she had to squint to get a better view. Dark walls, an overgrown garden, nailed up windows and doors. Nothing else was left of her childhood home. She should have sold it immediately back then upon the real estate agent's inquiry.

"Why did I take all that trouble only to come back? I should never have accepted this invitation", she whispered softly to herself. She heard a noise that sounded like footsteps on crunching gravel. When she leaned over and looked down, she detected a shadow running away. She quickly shut the window and slipped back into the partial shade of the room.

The Reception

There had been a flurry of activity in the mansion since the early morning. The gardener re-arranged the flowers on the terrace with the lady of the house and quietly discussed the advantages and disadvantages of geraniums.

Bernice and Harrison had set up a long table for the buffet in the dining room and chairs at the tables on the terrace. Along with the white wicker furniture, the rose arrangements on the tables and the large green parasols, everything looked tastefully decorative.

Phillis set the breakfast table for the guests in the salon, although she assumed nobody would even think of having breakfast at 11:00 a.m., that is, an hour before the reception. But Lady Fedora had issued these instructions and therefore she had no choice but to comply.

Beanstock and Mrs Argyle professionally monitored all the goings-on and only intervened when necessary. It promised to be a wonderful sunny day, as though especially ordained for the reception

Milady had planned. She was no longer so certain this reception had been such a good idea, but the invitations could not be withdrawn. Besides, the Earl of Southcoffelton was expected, accompanied by his wife; it was out of the question to make any changes. Filomena appeared and reminded Milady to change her outfit.

"How are things going with Miss Hillman? Weren't you assigned to be available for her?" Lady Fedora asked, slightly indignant over the interruption of her favourite pastime – toiling away in her prized flower garden.

"She excused me from of this obligation by pointing out that she would prefer taking care of her wardrobe and hair on her own instead of entrusting it to a clumsy country maid."

Lady Fedora raised her eyebrow, while her cheeks took on an unhealthy ruddiness. "Well, let's go upstairs and tend to my wardrobe for the reception. You have always been very capable in these matters, Filomena."

The two ladies hurried away.

Sir Percival was already appropriately dressed for the occasion in his light beige summer suit.

"Beanstock", he shouted. Junior immediately retreated to the salon.

"Sir Percival?"

"Where are our two house guests? The reception starts in half an hour and I want everything to proceed to my wife's satisfaction." Contrary to his typical behaviour, he whispered to the butler: "I will be overjoyed when both of them leave the day after tomorrow."

"Everything has been arranged to your satisfaction. Why don't you relax and enjoy the beautiful sunny day... I will take care of the rest. And if I may advise you, the aforementioned guests are still in their rooms." The butler bowed slightly and returned to the salon to assess the buffet arrangement.

Sir Percival looked around carefully before sneaking into the library. He quietly shut the door, picked up the decanter of whisky and reached for one of the glittering crystal glasses.

"Percival Parsley!" The loud shouting came from his wife, who was on her way downstairs, anxiously looking for him. He was surprised by her uncharacteristic yelling and nearly spilled the good whisky.

He took a large swig before joining his wife in the hall.

"How beautiful you look again today, my love", he complimented in an attempt to appease her.

Lady Fedora wore a light blue summer dress with a wide skirt and a narrow top with mid-length sleeves. The pattern of its light fabric consisted of dancing blue flowers and butterflies. Her London tailor had dispelled her concerns by assuring her this was *au courant* in London now. He had also wanted to entice her into wearing a matching hat, a strange concoction of beaded wire mesh with a leaf-shaped piece of leather on top and long white feathers protruding from the sides. Lady Fedora had been very amused and laughingly refused, whereupon her disgruntled tailor rolled his eyes in frustration.

The gravel in the driveway in front of the manor crunched loudly. Beanstock gingerly approached the door to see who had arrived.

A silver-grey limousine squealed to a stop after a precarious sudden turn, causing the gravel to scatter in all directions. One of the car doors flew open and a gentleman stepped out, grumbling all the while. Slightly older than Sir Percival, he wore a brown checked suit, had a huge twirled moustache, and wore a slightly crumpled brown light hat on his head.

"Do you even know how to drive? Next time we'll take the Jeep, instead or I'll get the chauffeur to drive the limo! Look at my new hat, this is what always happens with your confounded speeding!"

A smiling Gonzales had now opened the door at the driver's side to assist the Earl of Southcoffelton's wife out of the car. This was his responsibility today. He had again donned his best cap positioned over his black curls and the gold-coloured buttons shone on his jacket, which Beanstock observed with great satisfaction.

Lady Marjorie grinned cheerfully. "My dear Mortimer, your dreadful brown hat does not merit anything better, and you can't tootle around and be outrun by rabbits. You know that driving is my one great pleasure, so be good."

Lady Marjorie was a strong-willed lady with a penchant for fast cars. She and her husband owned a small estate in the neighbouring village complete with an old, draughty moated castle, which the Lord had inherited from his ancestors. They bred noble horses and small Dandie Dinmont terriers. As was suitable for her numerous activities, Lady Marjorie preferred to wear trousers since they were much more comfortable. Today her husband had persuaded her to put on a dress instead, which had not been easy for her. In the process of stepping out of the vehicle and handing the keys to Gonzales for parking, she self-consciously tugged at her lovely, bright summer dress as though it were too short.

The hosts appeared in the doorway and cheerfully welcomed their friends. The two couples had known each other for a very long time. Their families had maintained an amicable relationship for ages and were extremely fond of their mutual visits.

Rumour had it that the Earls of Southcoffelton and the Baronets Parsley had waged a lengthy, bloody battle centuries ago. Precious few documents were available and Sir Percival had been searching for proof of this old legend for a long time. In all likelihood they had battled over a fishpond, a bent suit of armour or a fallen lady who was said to have loved the sons from both families. No one could claim anything definite. Fortunately, the sword fights of old were long passé; at best, they only waged war with a knife and fork and a tough turkey now.

Lady Fedora had an affinity for the strong-willed Lady Marjorie and immediately linked arms with her.

"My dear Marjorie, we haven't seen each other for such a long time, this is not acceptable. We need to get together far more often. I have missed you terribly. Where are your daughters? Aren't they coming?"

"Oh, I hardly see them. As you know they're studying at Cambridge."

Lady Fedora caressed her friend's arm. "We shouldn't complain, but actually be glad that young women are finally allowed to pursue any field of their choosing. This hasn't always been the case, as you know. Remember how hard it was for me to convince my father I wanted to study art more than anything in the world?…"

Lady Fedora guided her friend into the house, across the hall and through the dining room onto the terrace. Phillis awaited the guests with glasses of sparkling champagne on a tray as they gradually arrived. The first – as was typical – were the pharmacist with his family.

His daughter Pamela wore a touch too much make-up and a brand-new purple dress that was so tight that it would certainly capture the gentlemen's fancy. The young girl was visibly excited as she surveyed the surroundings. They were warmly welcomed by the hosts and offered a glass of champagne. Mrs Hoppleton went out of her way to extend her gratitude for the invitation. For the sake of self-preservation, the pharmacist and his son Brian did not join their ladies: Brian had already greatly annoyed his sister at home by remarking she looked like a slatternly-dressed opera diva.

Shortly thereafter Mrs Bloom arrived on her garish green bicycle – thankfully without her tomcat, which accompanied her everywhere, as a rule. She was wearing a brand-new hat with various fanciful flowers that bounced on her head. To prevent it from flying away, she had tied a green bow not only around the hat but also under her chin, which Beanstock noticed with great bemusement.

Inspector Greenwood, the portrait of elegance in a blue double-breasted suit, brought Reverend Wilson along in his official car. The Inspector, a slim man with curly black hair and a thin moustache, was responsible for the northern area of the small county. He had been relocated about a year ago to a small police station in Parsley Field, very close to the railway station. His only employee, Constable Donegal, had been living here for some time and knew almost every inhabitant of the county personally.

Dr Winterbottom and his sister were the next

guests to arrive. The latter was very pretty yet very overwrought. The last arrivals were Mr Divari from the *Rosebud* Hotel and his secretary, Miss Summerset. The soft waves of her light blonde hair reached her shoulders and she wore a beautiful viridescent chiffon dress with a large collar.

"What a feast for the eyes", Lord Mortimer remarked, twirling his thick moustache. Mr Partridge's ears would surely turn red again at such a sight.

Mr Divari wore one of his traditional Indian robes, narrow white trousers, and a long white shirt with a high collar for the occasion. The only ornament was an elaborate gold-coloured braid around the neckline.

The guest of honour and the publisher were conspicuously absent.

"She'll no doubt be rehearsing her special stage appearance", Bernice whispered into Phillis' ear, both giggling softly. The two girls made the rounds with trays full of champagne glasses and offered them to the guests.

The guest of honour appeared in a fragrant cloud of vanilla – and a white trouser suit!

Lady Marjorie immediately shot a reproachful look at her husband. "And I had to put on this dress because you considered it proper."

Long pearl necklaces jingled on Inga's neck, her hair was combed and severely slicked back with gel.

Lady Fedora had to sit down. Sir Percival quickly

took over for her and introduced Inga Hillman. A few minutes later, the Baronets' second guest came slowly down the stairs. Beanstock noticed the dark circles under his eyes. Mr Van Horten positioned himself next to Miss Summerset and observed the hotel owner. Mr Divari bowed to Inga, hands folded and whispered, "Namaste, Priscilla, we haven't seen each other for a very long time."

"Please call me Inga, Davinder, I didn't expect to meet you here."

They spoke in hushed tones and went for a short stroll in the garden.

Miss Summerset clenched her fists at the spectacle. The Winterbottom siblings looked at each other in unmistakable confusion.

Mrs Bloom took another glass of champagne and immediately initiated a conversation with the pharmacist's wife, who also seemed quite displeased. Publisher Van Horten nervously drummed his fingers on his glass while housekeeper Mrs Argyle watched him in disgust.

Inspector Greenwood engaged in a discussion with Sir Percival and the Earl about the upcoming hunting season while Lady Marjorie admired Junior's excellent form.

The only ones who truly seemed to be enjoying themselves were the pharmacist and his son, Brian. They had snuck out of the house and joined Gonzales in gazing in awe at publisher Van Horton's Bugatti

Atalante.

Beanstock stood watching the party at the door to the dining room. A strange tension was in the air, which was evident by the guests' agitated facial expressions and furtive whispers. He had never experienced such a strange reception in his professional career. It almost appeared to him as though some of the guests were either slyly observing each other or feeling extremely ill at ease. The butler decided to invite the guests over to the buffet a bit earlier as a diversion. He approached Lady Fedora and informed her that dinner was ready to be served.

She graciously called on her guests to help themselves.

The guests made their way into the dining room, took their plates, and filled them with all the sumptuous dishes Mrs Porkpie had prepared. Her masterpiece, a three-tiered raspberry cream cake adorned with tiny marzipan roses, held court at the centre of the buffet.

Mulligatawny soup prepared according to an Indian recipe, jellied chicken, roast beef, crispy guinea fowl drumsticks, crusty bread, and a variety of mixed pickles from the cook's stockpile were also offered. Beanstock and the housekeeper served the beverages, as requested.

The first conspicuous stains on Reverend Wilson's soutane originated from the delicious soup. At the end of the meal, it was a custom to hazard a guess which food – and in which order – had been eaten based on the various stains found on the guest's clothes.

After a few minutes, Miss Hillman and Mr Divari rejoined the other guests. Beanstock noticed the pallor on the Indian's usually tanned face and observed Miss Hillman briskly moving away from him and initiating a conversation with Dr Rachel Winterbottom. But the brief exchange soon ended and apparently resulted in Dr Winterbottom's loss of appetite. She handed her filled plate to Phillis, who now looked beseechingly at Beanstock for help. He motioned for her to take the plate into the kitchen.

Rachel Winterbottom then approached her brother, whispered something in his ear and looked entirely unimpressed. Timothy Winterbottom responded by biting heartily into a juicy guinea fowl drumstick.

Rachel returned to the terrace with a glass of wine, her face pinched, sat down in one of the wicker chairs and gazed into the distance.

Beanstock increasingly became concerned at the bizarre goings-on.

Miss Hillman nibbled at a piece of jellied chicken, put the plate down on the large sideboard with a smile, took her golden cigarette case out of her trouser pocket, opened it, and withdrew a cigarette. She put the case aside and took a long golden cigarette holder from her other pocket. As she put the tip to her mouth, Mr Van Horten quickly joined her and held a lighter under her cigarette.

"What rude behaviour", the pharmacist's wife quietly remarked to her daughter, "I thought these elegant movie stars were paragons of good manners."

"It's obvious you only read the local papers, Mom, otherwise you would know that this *is* normal behaviour in such circles. I consider it wonderfully independent."

"And what does bad behaviour have to do with independence?" her mother asked in disgust. "Do you still want to be an actress?" Pamela set down her plate and strolled up to Miss Hillman. She briefly spoke to her and her cheeks reddened with excitement. Miss Hillman sized the girl up from head to toe, gave a reply with a smile and immediately abandoned her, whereupon Pamela was visibly reduced to tears.

Her brother Brian had noticed the sequence of events and spoke softly to her. He then took a handkerchief, wiped his sister's face and handed her his wine glass.

Beanstock had likewise observed the spectacle with mounting unease. He looked around for the second house guest, Mr Van Horten.

The butler hoped there would be no further problems, at least from this guest. The publisher was still standing at the sideboard, pouring himself a glass of the old whisky on hand. The butler would have liked to keep an eye on him, but was summoned by

Lady Fedora.

"Beanstock, do you also have the impression that the ambience here today is somewhat hostile? I actually intended to present my new book at the end of the reception. It is to be published in autumn. Mr Van Horten has the advance copy in his pocket, but doesn't seem pleased with it for some reason. And where is Miss Summerset? Mr Divari is ready to leave and asked me about her whereabouts. Why has our distinguished Mr O'Donoghue not shown up? I'm sure he would have saved the day with one of his amusing anecdotes. Why don't you try to clean the reverend's soutane? I think I'm going mad... Please *do* something, Beanstock!"

The butler sensed that Milady was beginning to lose patience with her guests.

"Lady Fedora, the beloved pub landlord has not excused himself, perhaps it's due to your celebrated godchild that he preferred to stay away". Lady Fedora looked at her butler with concern.

"He can't still be offended about that age-old story back then, can he? Good Lord, these men and their purported sense of honour, please excuse me, Beanstock."

At that moment Beanstock saw Miss Hillman come in and frantically looking around. He was about to inquire whether there was anything he could do to help when she hurried to the sideboard and picked up her cigarette case she had apparently left there. Mr

Van Horten took his whisky and went out onto the terrace. Beanstock noticed the astonishment on Bernice's face and observed the publisher with a perplexed gaze.

He walked up to her and asked, "Any problems, Bernice?"

The maid flinched.

"No, no, Mr Beanstock, everything is just fine." She hesitated for a moment. "I was just surprised that Mr Van Horten was helping himself to the whisky."

"He is a guest and it is not our duty to judge the guests' actions, no matter how strange they seem to be. Get back to your work."

Bernice curtsied and quickly went to the sideboard to arrange the glasses and decanters.

At that moment Miss Summerset returned from the garden and entered the dining room. Beanstock noticed her reddened cheeks. She immediately addressed her employer.

"Oh, you're ready to leave, Mr Divari. I apologise for keeping you waiting." The two said goodbye to the host couple, explaining they had important hotel business to attend to.

Their sudden departure prompted a mass exodus. All of a sudden, most of the guests were in a hurry and had urgent matters to settle. Only Lord and Lady Southcoffelton remained seated in their armchairs on the terrace, enjoying some excellent dessert wine and a sizable piece of Mrs Porkpie's delectable cake.

Meanwhile, there was a full-scale traffic jam in front of the main entrance since everyone had gotten into their cars simultaneously, anxious to leave. Beads of sweat were visible on Gonzales's forehead.

Finally, Inspector Greenwood stepped out of his official vehicle again and acted as a traffic cop, and soon the knot of cars began to untie and everyone sped off. The only guest who took more time to leave was Mrs Bloom on her bicycle.

In the interim, Lady Fedora dropped into an armchair next to Lady Marjorie, took a deep breath and ordered a whisky from Beanstock.

"Is everything all right, my dear?" Lady Marjorie asked.

"A splendid reception, Percival, I am pleased beyond measure, some interesting guests, to be sure", Lord Mortimer declared while removing cake crumbs from his beard.

"Yes, I know, Darling", his wife remarked, "you couldn't keep your eyes off the female guests. Now, finish your cake."

Lady Fedora looked around for her houseguests, particularly Inga, for whom this reception had actually been intended. She saw her godchild smoking and strolling in the garden. What had become of her publisher? She had no clue and closed her eyes in annoyance. Lady Marjorie looked at her anxiously.

In the meantime, Mrs Argyle had started to

allocate the tidying up duties in the dining room.

The remaining two guests had since said their goodbyes. Gonzales drove the car up and after doffing his hat, he opened the car door for Lady Marjorie with a slight bow.

"Thank you, Gonzales. Oh, Fedora", she turned to her friend, "do you realise what a lucky person you are? I think your staff is the best I've ever encountered. Just remember our last dinner party at our place. Our cook still can't bake a proper cake and Mortimer's butler? Well, you know what I mean. Due to his old age we are sometimes afraid he'll fall asleep before finishing a sentence. Recently, we actually caught him asleep in an armchair in the red salon, after we'd been waiting for our tea for a solid hour. So, my dear, chin up."

Lady Fedora managed to smile again. Her best friend always knew how to lift her spirits.

"Next time it's our turn to host the festivities. And bring cake. Fantastic whisky, my dear Percival", the Earl of Southcoffelton managed to shout before his wife revved the car's engine and lurched out of the driveway at a precarious speed.

By the time the two hosts returned to their house, all the furniture was back in place and Mrs Porkpie was busy preparing dinner in the sparkling clean kitchen.

Mr Van Horten came downstairs with Lady Fedora's new advance copy. Inga Hillman was in the hall, excused herself, claiming she had a headache, and went to her room.

Lady Fedora had tea brought to the salon and attempted to reason with her publisher, while her husband was finally able to go for a walk. He needed silence even more than Junior who now was beside himself with joy and bounded around him like a bouncing ball.

"It is *not* acceptable and I'm sticking to my guns. The book is perfect just as it is."

Lady Fedora stood wide-eyed in front of the window in their bedroom, arms crossed. After the tumultuous day, both of them were glad to finally retire to their comfortable bed. Sir Percival had been trying to calm his wife for several hours.

The discussion with her publisher had left her extremely upset.

"I still don't understand exactly what it is that displeases him, my dear", he commented while flipping through one of his old books.

His wife snorted. "It's the actual subject matter he dislikes. He complained that nobody in England would ever need an entire book about herbs and spices. As if they had no use at all. Even our ancestors recognised that herbs are essential for savoury dishes and to render foods more easily digestible. Considering that some people died while trying different plants, you'd think people would appreciate the compulsion to explore. In all likelihood it was pure chance that anyone learned how to use specific plants at all to achieve a certain flavour. Dill, parsley, cardamom, thyme, basil, cumin, ginger… The world would be much worse off without them."

Sir Percival looked up from his reading.

"Yes, and don't forget castor oil". Sir Percival whispered, rubbing his belly. "Darling, have you explained your sentiments to him the same way you've just done with me?" he asked.

"I was far too upset for that. I put our meeting off until tomorrow and apologised for the delay."

"As you've just explained to me, these are all good arguments in favour of this book. Your exposition would make for the perfect preface."

Lady Fedora looked at her husband in surprise.

"You're absolutely right. Why do I only realise these things after the fact? You are wonderful, darling!"

"It's never too late", her husband mused, dedicating his attention again to his book on the legends of the Norman era. His wife leapt out of bed, quickly donned her long, soft dressing gown, and put on her slippers.

"Where are you going?" her husband asked. "Possibly the kitchen…?"

A hopeful expression appeared on Sir Percival's face. He could already taste the cup of cocoa.

"What do you think? As you said, it's never too

late. I'm going to my studio to write down my arguments before I forget. I can't wait till tomorrow. And, Darling, you've had enough treats for today."

With these words, she scurried out of the room. As she quietly closed the door behind her, she heard the sound of soft sobbing from the direction of the guest rooms. She approached the room and knocked on Inga's door.

"Inga, my child, are you all right?"

The door opened a crack. Inga Hillman stood there in her long white silk nightgown and wiped her face with a cloth. Her eyes were bloodshot. The cigarette in her hand trembled. Lady Fedora pushed open the door the rest of the way and entered immediately.

"What happened, Inga?" she asked anxiously. "Is something wrong?"

"Please call me Priscilla, Aunt Fedora."

Large teardrops began rolling down her face again.

Lady Fedora impulsively hugged her, holding her close.

"Tell me what's bothering you."

"I should never have come here. All the terrible memories have come flooding back and I've alienated all the people who once meant a great deal to me. Whenever I look out the window, I see our house – and all these awful things start happening again."

Lady Fedora guided her to an armchair and poured

some water from the available carafe into a glass.

"It's true you've experienced hardships, yet you still managed to build your own life and you need to put these things behind you. The fate of your sister or your parents was not your fault. Everything will be fine, my child. And you know we're always there for you. Now calm down, I'll have a sleeping pill brought to you. You'll have a good sleep and everything will look brighter in the morning. Perhaps we should pay a visit to your house tomorrow. You need to properly say goodbye and sell everything in it. We'd be happy to help you. What do you think?"

Inga nodded and a slight smile appeared on her pale face.

"I guess I've made a spectacle of myself, haven't I? But you can't imagine what it's like in Hollywood. You have to be tough to get ahead. And when you get older...", Inga stopped and tears rolled down her cheeks again.

Lady Fedora stroked her head.

"Regardless, you're an exceptional actress."

She then went to the door where a bell directly connected to the butler and the staff area.

A few minutes later there was a soft knock. It was Beanstock, completely dressed in his uniform. She marvelled at the sight and pondered how he managed to look so perfectly attired in the middle of the night while he went to retrieve the requested sleeping pill from the medicine cabinet.

Inga sat at her dressing table and powdered her tear-stained face. While dejectedly scrutinising the first signs of deep wrinkles in the mirror, she reached for the drop-shaped green bottle bearing the name *Shalimar* in curved lettering and sprayed a subtle scent of vanilla on her décolleté.

She retrieved a cigarette from the golden case and gazed at the filigree lettering on its lid for a long while before lighting the cigarette. She took a deep drag, the smoke escaping from her mouth like light mist on an autumn morning.

When the butler returned, Lady Fedora put Priscilla to bed, gave her a small pill and tucked her in with care.

"You'll be able to get a proper night's sleep now. See you tomorrow."

Priscilla coughed slightly and closed her eyes, whereupon Lady Fedora left the room. The butler was waiting outside the door for any further requests.

"Go to bed, Beanstock. I apologise for the late disturbance, but I didn't want to leave the poor child alone."

"Good night, Milady."

Lady Fedora went to her studio to put a few thoughts in writing.

The butler stopped for a moment at the landing and turned his head upon hearing a noise. He wanted to ensure he was no longer needed. But it was silent. He went downstairs into the hall and confirmed that the door was locked before entering his room.

In the other guest room, Mr Van Horten quietly stepped back from the door; he had heard enough. He went to the window and opened it. The cool night air felt good as he deeply inhaled it.

Inspector Greenwood
Investigates

Beanstock's morning began as usual with his music and a proper cup of tea.

The previous day had raised many questions that were to be thoroughly discussed in the manor's kitchen. As long as the lordship's butler was not yet present, it was no problem to lighten up the morning with a bit of gossip. Mrs Argyle deliberately turned a blind eye and granted the staff some fun, especially as all of them had done such an excellent job the previous day. When the butler appeared, the employees present contentedly set off to their respective tasks. It was a day just like any other.

After the lord and ladyship had finished breakfast with Lady Fedora's publisher, Van Horten announced his plans to return to London as soon as possible and went to his room to pack.

Sir Percival was in his library. None of the guests were expected to make their presence known before noon.

Lady Fedora went to the garden to check up on the dill flowers and then have another talk with her publisher to sort out the previous day's clash of opinion. She walked through the salon to the terrace and briefly looked up at her godchild's windows. She hoped the young woman was feeling better today. Lady Fedora saw that the window was wide open. Last night's wind had quite likely caught a curtain and blown it out of the open window.

She returned to the house and called for Bernice. The girl appeared with a slight curtsy.

"Bernice, may I ask you to go to Miss Hillman's room? You are allowed to enter very quietly and close the window. The curtain got caught on the outside and could be damaged. I'm sure Miss Hillman will understand. It's already 10:00 a.m."

Bernice curtsied again and went upstairs without delay. She encountered Mr Van Horten next to the door to his room on the corridor of the guest wing and greeted him with a nod, whereupon he disappeared inside. She turned to the left and knocked very carefully on the door of the green room. No answer. She looked around to see if anyone was in the corridor and then put her ear to the door to hear whether Miss Hillman had already got up. She heard a groan. Bernice became frightened at the sound, so much so that it gave her goose bumps. She quietly opened the door.

Inga Hillman was lying on the floor just behind the door, as though she had attempted to reach the bell. She was still holding the small gold cigarette case in her hand, but lay completely still. Bernice started frenetically ringing the bell. The butler immediately arrived, accompanied by Mrs Argyle. Beanstock right away understood the urgency of the situation. He reached for the film star's neck and checked for a pulse. It was weak, but still detectable. Her breathing was intermittent and irregular, and her arms were cramped.

"Bernice, please help me carry Miss Hillman to the bed. Mrs Argyle, inform Milady at once and call Dr Winterbottom."

Lady Fedora and Sir Percival came and tried to rouse the young woman. Milady held her hand and began to tremble terribly.

"She is hardly breathing. What can we do?"

Fortunately, there were telephones, and Parsley Field was not very far. After less than ten minutes Dr Winterbottom was running up the stairs two steps at a time, his doctor's bag in tow. Beanstock instructed Bernice and Mrs Argyle to leave the room.

The doctor took his stethoscope and listened for his patient's shallow, intermittent breathing. He opened her eyelids and Beanstock noticed straightaway that her pupils were quite black and dilated. The doctor opened Inga's mouth and saw her swollen tongue covered with reddish pustules. Dr Winterbottom turned to Lady Fedora and her husband.

"Do you know if Miss Hillman has taken any

drugs? Or is she on any medication that you know of?"

Lady Fedora shook her head in response.

"Last night I gave her a mild sleeping pill because she seemed very agitated."

Dr Winterbottom filled a syringe. But before he could inject its contents, Priscilla's body seized up as though she were having a spasm. She tried to breathe and her eyes opened widely before she sank back onto the bed. Then followed an eery silence. The stilted breathing had stopped and Inga Hillman lay peacefully and lifelessly on the bed. Dr Winterbottom tried to resuscitate her, to no avail. A few moments later the doctor slowly and sadly rose from his patient's bed.

"I am very sorry, Milady, it's too late! There is nothing more I can do. She is dead."

Lady Fedora's hand tightly gripped her husband's arm. Her face turned white as a sheet. No one said a word.

Beanstock took her by the elbow and led her out with her husband.

In the hall, Lady Fedora's publisher waited beside his suitcase, ready to leave the manor.

"Is anything wrong, Sir Percival?" he asked with a concerned facial expression, only to be apprised of the terrible circumstances.

When Dr Winterbottom slowly made his way downstairs, the conversation abruptly stopped.

"So sorry to hear, but nevertheless I must leave now", the publisher announced and was about to take his suitcase.

"Beanstock, please take the luggage and bring it to Mr Van Horten's car", Sir Percival instructed in an unusually quiet voice.

"Pardon me, Sir Percival", the doctor interrupted him, "you must inform Inspector Greenwood. The cause of death is unknown and as such I cannot issue the death certificate at this time."

"Sir Percival, may I point out to you that Mr Van Horten ought to remain here under the circumstances. I'm certain the police will want to record his statement", the butler directed his words toward the baronet and noticed the publisher's reaction with a sidelong glance. Mr Van Horten had become visibly nervous.

Since Sir Percival was clearly overwhelmed and unable to cope with this situation, Beanstock telephoned Inspector Greenwood to inform him accordingly. He then instructed Miss Arbuckle to look after Lady Fedora who had since appeared in the salon.

The police car arrived shortly thereafter and fortunately, as Beanstock noticed, without the piercing wail of the siren.

Inspector Greenwood bent over the corpse and spoke in a quiet voice. His Constable, duly dressed in uniform according to regulations and sporting a neatly trimmed thick moustache, recorded his superior's observations word for word on his notepad. He intermittently licked the pencil tip and avoided looking at the deceased lady on the bed. Constable Donegal was green at the gills and various shades of red appeared on his cheeks. This was his first corpse.

The butler stood next to him, observing the official procedures. On the other side of the bed, Dr Winterbottom bent over the dead body and tried to explain the symptoms to the Inspector. In his opinion, the symptoms precluded a natural death.

"Upon my arrival, the patient was unconscious. Her breathing was intermittent and shallow. Her pupils were dilated, which may indicate intoxicants, drugs, or even poisoning. Her pulse was barely perceptible and she seemed to have a fever. Her hands were cramped, which is still evident. Her tongue was very swollen." With these words, the doctor pointed to the deceased woman's mouth with a pair of tweezers.

Inspector Greenwood cleared his throat. "Was Miss Hillman moved after she died?" he questioningly turned to the butler.

"Bernice found her on the floor right by the door. We thought it best to put her on the bed. I then immediately sent for Dr Winterbottom."

"And what is your conclusion, Doctor?" the Inspector asked.

"I would recommend an autopsy. At this juncture I

am not able to determine the exact cause, and since she was a healthy young woman, in my estimation, I will only be able to issue a provisional death certificate."

The Inspector nodded in agreement.

Dr Winterbottom retrieved his bag and went downstairs to the hall.

"Have you touched anything else here, Mr Beanstock?"

The butler's honour as a detective seemed to be violated and he replied indignantly, "Of course not, nothing is out of place here."

"Well, I guess not. Can you tell at this stage whether anything is missing from the room?"

"Hmm, you've got me stumped there. We should definitely consult Miss Arbuckle in this regard since she was instructed to look after our guest."

The Inspector looked at the butler with a smile.

"How about allowing ME to speak to Miss Arbuckle, then. Oh, and Mr Beanstock, please inform everyone in the house of what happened. I want to interview each person who was here. It goes without saying that everyone is obligated to stay until the situation at hand has been resolved."

He was visibly irritated at his Constable, who was still frenetically writing.

"Donegal, you needn't include my last remark."

The Constable continued writing before he realised his gaffe and looked at the Inspector with a wry grin. A bead of sweat dropped onto his freshly ironed uniform.

"The forensics team will be here in about an hour, and the corpse will be picked up. This room is not to be cleaned prior to the completion of interviews."

Mr Beanstock felt he was being patronised yet again. He pulled himself together and replied defensively, "Very well, Inspector."

The occupants of the mansion had gathered downstairs in the reception hall, and soft whispers interrupted the unnatural silence. Lady Fedora and her husband were in the salon as the Inspector came down from the upper floor. He informed Sir Percival of the facts at hand and asked for a quiet room in which he might conduct the interviews.

Mr Van Horten stood at the window with a cup of tea.

"Perhaps you would consider interviewing me first, Inspector. I have very important business in London to attend to", he explained in a tone that did not accept any argument.

"I am sorry, Mr Van Horten, even someone as important as you must remain until the cause of death has been determined", the Inspector replied.

Sir Percival slowly rose from his armchair, tenderly patted his wife's hand, and followed the policeman into the hall.

He attempted to put the staff at ease.

"Please remain calm and answer all the

Inspector's questions as precisely as possible." He then rejoined his wife.

The interviews were to take place in the library and Constable Donegal followed his superior self-importantly.

Knowing full well he would not be participating in the interviews, Beanstock elaborated a sophisticated ruse to nonetheless appear in the library. Books had to be fetched for the Baronet, tea was to be served to the Inspector – politely offered, of course – the windows were to be opened and then closed again without fail, Sir Percival's stationery was demanded since his paper was being used for the investigation. When he interrupted the policeman's interviews yet again, Inspector Greenwood waved his right hand in annoyance and said, "Good Lord, Beanstock, for heaven's sake just stay here and listen. There's no getting rid of you, is there?"

"Very well, Sir. Very well." With these words, the butler positioned himself contentedly next to the Constable who was industriously recording the details.

The servant and the gardener had been the first to be interrogated. It turned out that both of them had either been working outside or in their rooms. Beanstock could confirm that on the previous day Harrison had immediately disappeared into his room upon completion of the cleaning duties.

The housekeeper was the next to be interviewed.

She was visibly distraught and had to continually wipe away the tears that kept welling up. She reported not to have witnessed anything unusual, briefly glancing at Mr Beanstock during her testimony, and asserted that once she had fulfilled her duties she retired for the night around 10:00 p.m.

The interview with the cook proceeded similarly. Inspector Greenwood paid special attention to her, demanding every detail regarding how she had prepared the food. Mrs Porkpie angrily crossed her arms in defiance.

"Are you insinuating that my food was tainted? In my many years of working for the Baronet and his wife, no one has ever complained or died after eating my food."

The butler cleared his throat.

"Mrs Porkpie, I think the Inspector only wants to ensure that no one tampered with it. You understand, don't you? Nobody is accusing you. Samples of the food will surely be needed, won't they, Inspector?" He regarded the policeman with interest.

"Yes, food samples would definitely be necessary", the latter hastened to agree with him.

"I'll see to it straightaway", Mrs Porkpie hissed between clenched teeth. The cook stood up, took a deep breath, scowled at the Constable, and rushed out of the room. Constable Donegal lost his train of thought and had to search his notes. What had he just written down? He read the last note to be "Samples of food required", shook his head and crossed out the last sentence.

Filomena Arbuckle was next to be interviewed. She explained that Miss Hillman had sent her away, and that she had not encountered her again after that. Further, she could not ascertain whether anything was missing from the deceased woman's room.

The chauffeur reported all vehicle arrival times, their respective license plates as well as the interesting car models. His only other contribution was to claim not to know anything more. Inspector Greenwood focused attention on his Constable once again, this time in annoyance upon noticing that he was zealously recording all the vehicle models.

Phillis could not supply any details since she had spent most of the time in the kitchen with Mrs Porkpie or in her room, nor had she noticed anything untoward during the reception the day beforehand. Instead of providing any useful information, she made eyes at the Constable which once again garnered an admonishment from Beanstock. Phillis left the interrogations with a curtsy, whereupon Mr Van Horten appeared in the doorway and demanded to be interviewed immediately, claiming he had better things to do than to wait in the hall with the staff. These very circumstances were an unnecessary affront and a nuisance to him.

The Inspector invited him into the room and Beanstock closed the door with a quick glance down the hall. Bernice was the only one still waiting in the area. In that brief moment he noticed she was pacing, muttering something unintelligible under her breath and seemed completely lost in thought.

Mr Van Horten did not deign to await the Inspector's questions.

"I am a guest in this house and I have never seen Miss Hillman before. I only briefly met her for the first time the night prior to the reception. She retired to her room, claiming she wasn't feeling well. Unless I'm mistaken, Inspector, you were here on Saturday and thus do not require a further report of this boring story. Besides, the only reason I'm here at all was to discuss details for Lady Fedora's book. I went to my room early yesterday evening in order to get some sleep as I intended to return to London early today. I didn't hear anything unusual. If there is any other information you require from me, you can consult my solicitor in London."

The Constable had to stop for a moment to wiggle his cramped fingers after such intense writing, yet could only barely keep up.

Beanstock listened in amazement. Mr Van Horten had certainly conjured up a good story.

Inspector Greenwood smiled.

"Well, thank you very much for your statement. I will be in contact should any further information be required."

The publisher stood up and hastened out of the

library. Beanstock looked with interest at the Inspector to find out whether he likewise found it strange. But Beanstock could not ascertain any reaction; the Inspector's demeanour was inscrutable.

Apart from Beanstock, Bernice was the last of the manor personnel to be interrogated. Beanstock summoned the maid on his own accord. As he peered down the hall, he noticed Mr Van Horten was speaking with her and appeared angry. The butler called for Bernice who immediately came running, looking around uneasily.

"Are you all right?" he asked her anxiously.

But the girl ignored him and sat down in the chair in front of the Inspector.

"Alright, Bernice, you're the maid in this mansion. Please tell me where you were this morning and last night, let's say once the reception was over. I think we can safely ignore the actual reception since I was also there and even I didn't notice anything out of the ordinary."

It seemed to Beanstock as though Bernice had breathed a sigh of relief after the Inspector's opening salvo.

She put on record that activities at the manor had been the same as usual and that she turned in for the night at 10:00 p.m. Since the butler had heard Bernice and Filomena, her whereabouts could be verified.

The next morning, according to Lady Fedora's instructions, she had checked the curtains in Miss

Hillman's room and discovered her lying on the floor. She immediately rang for the butler and was later requested to leave the room. She had nothing further to add to her statement. The inspector let the maid go. Now only Beanstock's statement was still missing.

"The evening turned out as expected. The Baronets' guests as well as her ladyship and Sir Percival turned in early for the evening right after dinner. When I'd finished tidying up, I went to my room where I not only heard one of the servants snoring, but also Filomena and Bernice chattering as they came upstairs. I went to bed to read for a while. At around 11:00 p.m. Milady rang the bell connected to my room to call for me. I dressed as quickly as possible. Lady Fedora was in Miss Hillman's room and seemed very upset. She asked for a sleeping pill from the medicine cabinet, which I fetched straightaway."

At this juncture of the testimony the butler noticed the Inspector and his Constable exchanging a knowing glance.

Beanstock continued with the sequence of events.

"I then checked the front door again to ensure it had been properly locked before returning to my room. ... When Bernice found Miss Hillman in distress this morning, I immediately sent for Dr Winterbottom."

Inspector Greenwood rose.

"And you did not notice any signs of forced entry

when you came downstairs this morning?" Beanstock replied in the negative.

The Inspector announced he would briefly interview the Baronets in the salon.

Lady Fedora sat hunched over in one of the brightly coloured armchairs. Her hands involuntarily clenched when the Inspector appeared.

"Lady Fedora, I've just heard that you gave Miss Hillman a sleeping pill last night. Is this true?" Milady nodded in confusion.

"And you asked your maid to check up on Miss Hillman this morning? Is this also true?" Milady nodded again in the affirmative.

At that moment, Beanstock could already guess the Inspector's train of thought and interrupted him.

"Do you mean to suggest that this pill is the cause of the young woman's death? And that Milady deliberately precipitated it? You can't be serious. It was a simple, ordinary, mild sleeping pill. We don't have any high-dosage medication in this house. I gave that tablet to Milady straight from the package. And the curtain had got caught on the outside of the window, which is the reason Bernice went upstairs in the first place."

Lady Fedora turned extremely pale. Sir Percival watched his wife anxiously.

"Are you implying she deliberately wanted to harm our godchild? How can you say such a thing?" he asked hoarsely.

The Inspector raised his hands defensively.

"No, I'm not claiming anything of the sort, please don't get upset. Suffice it to say, however, we must wait for the autopsy report. But please understand that I am obligated to investigate every angle. I must ask everyone present to remain available until the cause of death is determined", the Inspector replied.

The head of the forensics unit returned from the upper floor and reported they were finished. He handed a forensics bag to the Inspector. The body of the movie star had already been removed.

"Were you aware Miss Hillman was using drugs?" Inspector Greenwood asked everyone in the room while holding up the forensics bag. Lady Fedora shook her head in utter disbelief and shock.

"This seemingly innocuous white powder has caused misfortune to many people, although it doesn't appear dangerous at first glance. Well, we'll see", he quietly contemplated as he put the bag in his jacket pocket.

The sound of squealing brakes was heard in front of the house. The front door was wrenched open, followed by hastily approaching steps.

Mr Divari appeared in the doorway of the salon, wide-eyed with disbelief.

"This must surely be a mistake! Tell me it isn't true, Sir Percival. She was completely fine yesterday, wasn't she? Or was she actually ill?" He sank into an armchair in shock at the sight of Lady Fedora's sorrowful eyes.

"Incredible how efficient the rumour mill operates around here", Inspector Greenwood muttered.

"The cause of death is still unknown. What was your relationship to the deceased?"? he asked with interest.

The Indian looked up, tears glistening in his eyes.

"A very long time ago we were secretly engaged, which is a sad story. I spoke to Priscilla on the day of the reception and assured her I still loved and adored her. I tried to explain why things didn't work out between us back then. My family forced me to break off the engagement. We were still far too young and foolish at the time. How different both of our lives would have turned out if I had been courageous enough to stand up to my family. But she told me in no uncertain terms yesterday that she had got over me long ago."

He buried his face in his hands and bitterly sobbed.

"How could this have happened?" the Indian asked, looking around in dismay.

Sir Percival glanced at his butler and gestured for him to bring some tea. Beanstock bowed briefly and left. Various thoughts sprung to mind as quickly as startled butterflies. He had to make sense out of this chaos. At this point it was likely his duty to do so; he couldn't leave it up to the Inspector, otherwise it would be only a matter of time before an innocent man would be accused and hanged. He had the vague feeling that the reception had not gone off as innocuously as the Inspector assumed. Yet the latter had ignored his hint on the matter at hand. He decided to speak to every guest again who had attended the reception – and especially the staff.

Someone had to know something, even if they did not realise it yet. But first things first: he had to explain to the housekeeper in no uncertain terms that this was not the time for harbouring secrets.

When he entered the kitchen, there was a silence that he would have ordinarily welcomed on any other day. But today the bewildering quiet seemed oppressive. Even Gonzales was not in the mood to regale the household with his illustrious jokes. Mrs Porkpie kept wiping her eyes with a handkerchief, while Bernice and Phillis were standing stock-still and ghostly pale in the corner.

"Phillis, please make some tea." The kitchen maid quietly took the tea and silver pot out of the cupboard.

"Where is Mrs Argyle?" the butler asked the staff.

"She is in her office, Sir", Gonzales murmured.

"Bernice, please serve the tea to the guests. We require six cups. Do you feel up to it?" She nodded.

"That's a good girl." With these words, the butler left the kitchen and went into the adjoining hallway where he knocked on the door to housekeeper's office.

"Come in", was heard through the door.

Beanstock entered the room and gingerly closed the door behind him. He wanted to be sure no one would overhear even one word of their conversation.

"I've been expecting you", Mrs Argyle said, standing up from her chair in front of the bureau. She held the stack of letters in her hand that had yellowed over time, on top of which was the letter that had terribly unsettled her.

"Well, Mrs Argyle, I think you should come clean, our ladyship is in danger. The Inspector indeed suspects Lady Fedora."

The housekeeper was visibly startled and immediately sat down again.

"He can't actually be serious, can he?"

"You must tell me the absolute truth now. I promise to be discreet about anything you divulge and not to put you in any danger." Beanstock pulled up a chair and sat down.

"Does the acronym MI6 mean anything to you?" Beanstock nodded. She hesitated as if gathering her thoughts. "Back then, before I came to Parsley Manor, I worked for an unmarried gentleman. His name was Kim Philby. How would I describe him...? Let's say he kept a lot of secrets. He worked for His Majesty's Secret Service, in a manner of speaking. I was young and foolish at the time and got involved in a situation which you'll undoubtedly deem reprehensible. I became *very* close to my employer."

She swallowed and looked down at her hands, kneading them like dough.

"Well, when you become intimate with someone, you tend to pick up a few things that aren't meant for outsiders. Especially not for a mere employee, which I was at the time. He had studied at Cambridge in the 1930s and still had extensive connections there. One day, a former fellow student paid him a visit. It was Mr Van Horten." She looked pointedly at Beanstock for a moment.

"But, then…", she faltered.

"Mrs Argyle, please be assured that I will not betray your confidence. Besides, it is not my place to judge. If you believe anything could change the high opinion I have of you, you are wrong. So please continue."

She nodded while wiping a tear from her eye. "He introduced himself by a different name. I can remember it as if it were yesterday. Even back then he already was an arrogant pillock. Excuse me, Mr Beanstock. He went by the name Dr Richard McLean in those days and worked as a psychiatrist in *Bedlam* after graduating from Cambridge. Have you ever heard of it?"

The butler's eyes narrowed with strain. "I know it by its official name, *Bethlehem Royal Hospital*, but yes, I have heard of it. Some of the conditions were quite adversarial back then."

The housekeeper nodded. "At any rate, my former

employer was not very pleased to see him. I overheard arguments and the loud voices were unmistakable. They had to do with experiments in the clinic and matters of warfare.

Dr McLean submitted papers about his research pertaining to chemical weapons. The word Russia was mentioned. When I asked if dinner could be served, I noticed my employer's ashen face. His guest had already left the house. Then everything happened very quickly. He advised me to pack up all my belongings immediately. He went to his bedroom and packed as quickly as he could. All told, it took about fifteen minutes.

I was completely clueless. He gave me money, recommended I go to a hotel and then leave London. It was 1944. I didn't hear from him again for a long time. Fortunately, I was given the opportunity to start a new life with the Baronets here. Then I started receiving these letters."

Mrs Argyle handed the butler the stack of yellowed envelopes and Beanstock instantly recognised the Cyrillic letters on the postmark.

"He hightailed it to *Russia*? Was he a double agent?" The butler's voice nearly failed in his astonishment.

Mrs Argyle nodded.

"He belonged to a group which – as it is assumed – regularly met at Cambridge during his studies. Nobody knows who else was involved in it. Be that as it may, the doctor was a member of this particular group and he didn't just conduct experiments for England. This letter I received was posted right here in England. Which suggests he's since returned. He has severed all previous ties and has tried to lead a normal life. Please do not mention his name. He warned me against the doctor. His contacts are still active and he knows this man is Her Ladyship's publisher. That's the reason he wanted to warn me about Mr Van Horten, who is truly an evil and volatile man. Fortunately, this arrogant individual didn't recognise me. In those days, Philby was working for MI6 as a liaison for the BBC. In one of his letters he explained to me why everything had to happen in such a hurry.

Doctor McLean and his brother Donald McLean wanted to sell highly sensitive research results to the Russians and Kim robustly disagreed. He also knew that the doctor illicitly experimented on his patients with a chemical agent that could become essential for warfare. Kim had stumbled on the doctor's clandestine activities and couldn't go back. But he also knew it was only a matter of time before this activity would be exposed, and for this reason, he disappeared. Chance is a mean devil, isn't it? And now here, in the countryside, my past has caught up with me."

The housekeeper sighed.

"Do you think I should have told you earlier? Yet I

still cannot fathom someone like Van Horten being involved in the murder, can you? He didn't even know Miss Hillman at all – or did he?"

Beanstock stood up.

"Of that I am not yet certain. The question remains whether Mr Van Horten ought to be reported to counter- intelligence. But in that case, my dear Mrs Argyle, you could be implicated. And I am not willing to do that. First, I must clarify the facts and wait for the post-mortem results – that is, if this policeman will even deem me worthy of the information. We'll know more then. You're not to blame, Mrs Argyle. Don't you worry about a thing. Did you ever actually reply to those letters?"

"Never, I wouldn't even entertain the notion. Not to mention, I didn't have his address. I'm hard-pressed to understand why he still remembers me."

"Actually, I understand, my dear Mrs Argyle."

With these uplifting words, Beanstock left the disheartened housekeeper and went to the salon. In the meantime, Phillis and Bernice had served tea to everyone present, whereupon Beanstock sent them back to the servants' quarters.

The Small Shiny Object

How beautifully it shone. When she held it up to the light of the torch, she noticed the splendidly intricate detail on its surface. Although she knew full well that she was not allowed to keep it, she wanted to feel like an elegant lady or a movie star – even for just a moment. She carefully opened the lid. The intensely fragrant cigarettes in the case resembled small, white fingers with a golden tip. She very gingerly held them up to her face and inhaled their aroma with a smile. The faint scent of *Shalimar*, a famous perfume renowned for its typical vanilla notes, emanated from the case. She recognised this fragrance: the movie star had worn it and she remembered noticing the beautiful green-hued bottle on her dressing table.

She then closely examined the inside of the case which was embossed with the words, *To my cherished I. H. from E. F.* in exquisite penmanship. She had never owned anything as fancy as this before, and it pained her to have to leave it behind.

A noise in her proximity startled her. She quickly looked out from behind the tree, but could not see a soul. She then heard a loud crackling sound from the other side, as though someone had stepped on a dry branch. She peered up at the house which suddenly appeared dark and forbidding to her.

She closed the small shiny object and was about to return it to the box with the other items she had stashed there, away from the prying eyes of the others. The deep crevice in the old chestnut tree stalwartly kept her secret. Filomena in particular always begged to be in on every little detail and continually bombarded her with questions. But this secret hideaway was hers and hers alone.

After a brief moment of contemplation she decided to reopen the case. There would surely be no harm in trying another cigarette, since the first one had tasted so wonderful.

There were four remaining in the case; nobody would even notice that one was missing. And she could inhale the scent that symbolised a world to which she would otherwise never gain entrée.

After cautiously taking out a cigarette, she returned the case to the faded wooden box with its dark red rose on the lid along with her other treasures and fastened the lock into place. The box lay next to a silk scarf — the only memento she had of her mother — a cinema ticket, a wide, black velvet ribbon, a rusty key and a cheap pink ring from a candy machine.

If everything went without a hitch according to her dreams, she would soon no longer have to scour floors or serve tea. She would go to London and be able to live there without any notion of tomorrow. She tried to imagine what it would be like to live the good life in a flat of her own. It would be far better than the lost years with her aunt, who had made her feel unwanted day by day and constantly reminded her that by virtue of her generosity she was spared from a life in the orphanage and thus forever indebted to her.

To be sure, Parsley Manor was not the worst place to be employed, but she ultimately wanted to be independent, and to not have to constantly follow instructions. She coughed slightly. Suffice it to say, servants were not allowed to smoke in the house, either.

She sometimes sneaked off to Gonzales' place. He always had one of those frightfully strong Spanish cigarillos for her. She had to smile at the mere thought of her mortifying coughing fit the first time.

She took the matches from her apron pocket and sat down again, leaning against the trunk of her tree, her secret hiding place.

She deeply inhaled the smoke which also caused a cough, but one that would usually subside after the first few puffs. She looked up at the dark starry sky and envisioned her fabulous new life.

An owl screeched out a warning call into the night air to the nearby mice in preparation for its evening prowl. The sound of rustling could be heard next to

Bernice.

But she was oh so tired. All of a sudden, she found it difficult to breathe. Had she caught a fever? Her eyes were burning. It must have been the smoke to which she was not yet accustomed. She felt terribly ill and her pulse was racing.

She was utterly powerless to stand up or scream. Her eyes slowly became leaden and lifeless. Her last thought was that it had been a mistake to believe she could claw her way out of her station in life.

She regretted not confiding her observations at the reception to the butler that day. Nevertheless, her major misstep was most likely assuming she could purloin this shiny little object without any repercussions.

The gardener was smiling from ear to ear as he opened the door to the garden. He deeply inhaled the pure morning air and made his way to the kitchen for a proper breakfast. He rubbed his hands in giddy anticipation at the prospect of Mrs Porkpie's freshly baked raisin scones.

Mortecai emerged from the door behind him. He yawned and stretched laboriously before quickly following his friend and food provider.

As Mr Herringbone crossed the old orchard, he caught sight of something quite bewildering: Why on earth was Bernice sitting under a tree in the garden at this hour? As he approached her to ascertain whether she might have fallen asleep, he noticed her large, diluted, lifeless eyes and ashen face.

"Oh my God, that poor young thing", he gasped in horror.

Mortecai appeared from behind him to sniff at the girl. The gardener took him into his arms and hastened to the back kitchen door.

Mrs Argyle immediately sent for Mr Beanstock, who was still in his room listening to music. By the time he reached the tree, the rest of the servants were already in the yard encircling it. Mrs Arbuckle sobbed and rubbed her eyes until they were red. The butler bent over Bernice and closed her open, vacant eyes before he shooed everyone back into the house by way of a hand movement.

"Stay here Mr Harrison, if you don't mind, under the circumstances. I must inform Sir Percival and call the police once again", Beanstock turned to the servant.

Harrison nodded awkwardly while attempting to position himself next to Bernice with some semblance of decorum. He tried to stand on her left and to her right, then with crossed arms and arms dangling at his side and was visibly becoming unsure of himself. Beanstock watched his blundering behaviour for a short while.

"Harrison, just stand over there casually and think about nothing."

"And how does one think about nothing, Mr

Beanstock?"

The butler was about to turn around and return to the house to report the recent death when he noticed a stain. He bent over the girl and upon closer examination he noticed a round burn mark on the apron where her hand was resting in her lap. She might have gone out for another cigarette, the butler tried to justify to himself. He searched for a cigarette stub next to the dead woman.

But there was none.

The forensics team would surely be able to recover it, Beanstock hoped. Nevertheless, he would draw the Inspector's attention to the cigarette burn mark, no matter how cross it would make him. After contacting the police station, he called for Filomena Arbuckle. They went up to the first floor and the butler knocked softly on the door to the Baronets' bedroom.

Sir Percival's slightly tousled head of hair appeared at the door shortly afterwards.

"Please be quiet, she's finally fallen asleep. I could barely manage to calm her down last night", Sir Percival whispered and cast a worried glance at his wife who was lying pale and careworn in the large bed.

"What's the matter? What time is it, Beanstock?"

"I beg your pardon, Sir, it's 6:30 a.m. I regret to inform you that another corpse has been found."

"What? Who?" Sir Percival murmured as quietly

as he could.

"It's Bernice, her body's in the orchard behind the house. I have already taken the necessary measures", the butler elaborated.

Sir Percival wiped cold sweat from his forehead.

"Oh my God, what's going on here, now the poor young girl is also dead."

Lady Fedora appeared like a pale apparition in the doorway.

"I heard you. Don't bother keeping your voice down, Darling. Who would be playing such a malicious game with us, Beanstock?"

"Milady, at this point I cannot say, but I will surely do my utmost to find out. I brought Filomena to look after you."

The maid went into the bedroom and grabbed Lady Fedora's arm since she appeared as though she was incapable of keeping herself upright. Sir Percival went to his dressing room.

Beanstock could already hear the unmistakable wail of the police car siren. Great, now all the residents of Parsley Field would know that something terrible had happened at the Baronets' again. It would not surprise him in the least if in addition to the postman, the other village residents would also make an earlier appearance at the manor today.

Not to mention the matter of the press. Above all, the film star's death would be exploited in all its gruesome details. He had already had to answer several calls yesterday, all of which attempted to pump him for information. It was only a matter of time until the media hordes would arrive at the mansion. But he would figure out in due course how to stave off the unnecessary hysteria for his Lord and Ladyship. Go ahead: let the sensationalist vultures descend on us.

The official car of the Parsley Field police station squealed to a stop in front of the entrance. What would spring to the Inspector's mind this time regarding the murder?

The butler adjusted his waistcoat and jacket in preparation for another visit from the Inspector and his Constable who had a penchant for overzealously writing.

Poison

Once the residents of Parsley Manor had been interviewed again, the Inspector had explained to the Baronets Parsley in the butler's presence that according to the post-mortem report, Miss Hillman's death could have only been caused by poison. As a consequence, the case was now being treated a murder investigation. The coroner could not yet pinpoint the poisonous agent used; more tests would be necessary. But it had to have been a poison that was inhaled, since nothing could be found in the stomach of the victim, whereas an abundance of residues were detected in the lungs and blood. Miss Hillman had ultimately perished from acute respiratory failure.

Lady Fedora closed her eyes in abject sorrow.

"Poor child. What a horrible death."

The Inspector continued to explain that none of the pills examined or the food in Inga Hillman's stomach provided any evidence of poison, although the condition of the lung tissue clearly led to this conclusion. Of this verdict the coroner felt very confident, and as such they found themselves back at square one of the investigation.

"Nevertheless, I have informed our lawyer in London to this end. We expect his arrival in the next few hours", Sir Percival told the Inspector.

"As you wish, although I have no reason to suspect Lady Fedora at the moment. And now we must wait for the coroner's report regarding the maid. In addition, I would like to ask for your consent to search the house again. Although we do not know the type of poison, I would like to evaluate all the possibilities beforehand, which means the inventory of rat poison, the gardener's supplies of plant poison and so on", Inspector Greenwood explained and then stood up. He took a nervous sidelong glance at his eager Constable, who was frenetically writing down his every word.

"Donegal, you should just..." He interrupted himself as he watched his Constable continue writing and rolled his eyes at the sight.

Lady Fedora awkwardly got to her feet.

"Inspector, I don't blame you for implicating me; it's your job. We will gladly permit you to investigate anything you deem necessary, regardless that I already know our lawyer would not recommend this course of action. But we have nothing to hide here.

When can we lay Priscilla Hillman to rest? We'll be taking care of the funeral arrangements; she didn't have any relatives. Her aunt in London died three years ago and it is only proper to bury her here, alongside her parents and sister."

The Inspector nodded in agreement.

"I will inform you as soon as the coroner has completed his examination, Milady."

He nodded to everyone present.

The Inspector then proceeded to the orchard to survey the new crime scene again.

Sir Percival reached for his wife's hand and stroked it gently.

"Beanstock, please have some tea served and ask Mrs Argyle to come see us. She was the one who hired Bernice and would likely have information about her relatives. It would be wise to tend to these details before the policemen do, don't you agree?"

"Of course, Sir, I'll see to it straightaway."

The butler entered the kitchen where an awkward silence prevailed.

Herringbone had retired to his greenhouse after being interrogated by the police.

Mrs Porkpie leaned against her cooker, continuously shaking her head as though attempting to solve a difficult conundrum. Filomena embraced Phillis, who was sobbing inconsolably. Gonzales was in the garage, loudly rumbling with his tools while apparently trying to grasp why sweet Bernice would now be gone forever.

Harrison was sitting at the table. His big, strong hands were shaking.

"Has the girl already been removed from the crime scene?" Beanstock asked the servant while putting on water for the tea.

Harrison nodded without saying a word.

While the water was still boiling, Beanstock knocked at the housekeeper's door.

She opened and gave him a knowing nod.

"I found the documents pertaining to Bernice. I thought we might need them."

The butler sent her off to the Baronets, documents in tow, and then returned to make tea. When he entered the kitchen, Phillis had already made the preparations, including the tea tray. The butler gave her a thankful nod and carried the tray into the salon.

He noticed Mr Van Horten talking on the phone in the hall; he sounded very displeased. When he heard the butler approaching, he abruptly ended the call and went upstairs to the bedrooms without so much as a backward glance.

Very strange, the butler thought to himself, though it might have been an easily explainable phone call, wherein the publisher was consulting with one of his employees in London.

He had not set out to judge the man's every action, but instead opted to approach the matter with an open mind. Beanstock had to do something. He couldn't wait any longer. His criminal instincts told him to start his investigation among the reception guests. Something had to have happened that day that triggered this tragic series of events.

He decided to ask Sir Percival for the use of his car; he didn't wish to bother Lady Fedora.

After tea was served, Sir Percival went to his beloved library.

Beanstock knocked at his door.

Sir Percival sat in the large leather armchair reading one of his massive ancient history books.

Next to him was Junior, his head resting on the Baronet's knee, as though he sensed there was something amiss and needed to comfort his master. Lost in thought, Sir Percival patted his head.

"Where would you want to go, my good Beanstock?" the Baronet asked.

The butler was reluctant to let his employer in on his plan, but lying to him was even more unconscionable.

"Well, Sir, I'd like to ask some people a few simple questions."

"Hmm, what do you hope to discover? Surely you don't intend to interfere with the Inspector's investigation, do you? Beanstock, I must say that compared to a murder, a missing bottle of burgundy and a lost fountain pen are quite a different matter. And now there are two deaths. With all due respect concerning your detective skills, this pursuit seems dangerous to me, and I don't want any more trouble with the Inspector. But above all, I don't want you to be exposed to any danger. We don't know if there's a madman on the loose out here. Who are you planning to question?"

Beanstock felt uneasy and took a deep breath before responding.

"I want to find out more details about this strange reception and hope to shed some light on it. There must be somebody who saw something peculiar that day."

"So you think something happened during the reception? But I was also there and I didn't notice anything amiss. It was actually quite enjoyable, don't you think? I conversed with Lord Southcoffelton about the upcoming hunting season and about his dog breeding, didn't I, Junior, my good boy?" He turned to his dog with a smile. The beagle wagged his tail in acknowledgement.

"Pardon my candour, Sir, but the atmosphere was not exactly festive among the guests yesterday. Except perhaps for Lord and Lady Southcoffelton. A peculiar tension was in the air which I could not pinpoint. In order to get a clearer picture of the situation, I would like to interview the guests and have access to the car and enlist Gonzales accordingly. That is, unless you have any objections, Sir."

Sir Percival slowly stood up and nodded at him.

"While I truly appreciate your commitment, Beanstock, I must ask you to please tread very carefully. We should by no means annoy our fellow residents with any unfounded suspicions. I hope we can all soon return to our normal lives. Have you apprised the Inspector of your suspicions?"

"Yes, I have, Sir, but he has eliminated any association to that end."

The butler bowed slightly and left the library.

After issuing instructions to Mrs Argyle and re-allocating the day's tasks, he made his way to the garage where a rumbling cacophony could still be heard.

He opened the garage door and a completely oil-smeared face emerged from the open bonnet of an old Ford.

"Mr Beanstock? Maldito, has anyone else died?" the chauffeur asked with fearful eyes as he crossed himself.

The butler raised his hands.

"Don't worry, Gonzales, I just need the Bentley. I have to investigate a few things at Parsley Field. Sir Percival has granted his permission. If I could kindly ask you to chauffeur me, it's been a long time since I was allowed to drive an automobile."

"Okay, just give me a minute, Señor."

Gonzales went next door, where he removed his dirty overalls and replaced them with clean trousers and a fresh shirt. The butler heard the sound of water rushing. A much cleaner chauffeur appeared, took the keys from the rack and went into the second garage next door with the silver-grey Bentley.

"We'll go to the Winterbottoms first, Gonzales, unless you deem otherwise."

"*Dios mio*, Señor, are you always so formal?" Gonzales asked as he started the engine.

Beanstock looked at his chauffeur uncomprehendingly.

"Formal? I'm actually being perfectly normal."

The Spaniard shrugged his shoulders and drove off towards Parsley Field.

Shortly after the two had disappeared behind the trees, Mr Van Horten left the manor and walked down the front garden path in the direction of the fields.

Ghosts of the Past

It was an ordinary weekday at the Winterbottom siblings' surgeries. As was customary during the consultation hours, Simon Partridge, Phillis' older brother and the postman's son, was sitting at the reception desk in the anteroom.

The young man with curly blond hair was wearing a dazzling white coat. Contrary to his sister Phillis, he was tall and rather thin. The circular-lensed glasses perched on his nose tended to constantly slide down and then balance precariously on the tip of his nose. Simon's left hand often automatically shot up to his glasses and pushed them back into place without him being any the wiser.

The patients had initially considered it rather unusual to be welcomed by a male nurse, but in the course of time even the last of the sceptics had become accustomed to it.

Simon had wanted to become a doctor, and since it was difficult for his parents to raise the money for his studies, he decided to take the lengthy and arduous training as a nurse's apprentice. Due to his exceptionally good performance, he was a prime candidate for a scholarship. Until then, he received patients at the surgery, applied bandages, soothed the pain of crying children or calmed nervous pregnant women.

For the animal ward of the surgery, he recorded predominantly four-legged patients on the index cards and ensured they were admitted in the proper order.

Heaven forbid if stationmaster Templar's dachshund was called before Mrs Pommerton's budgie. After all, Mrs Pommerton always was the first and in fact already waiting outside the door, her covered cage in tow, before Simon even unlocked the waiting room.

But Simon competently managed the patient load without fail, as Dr Rachel Winterbottom could attest to on his behalf. He was expert at dealing with the sensitivities of small and large patients alike, and had thus made himself indispensable.

When Mr Beanstock entered the doctor's office that morning, all gazes immediately rested on him with unmasked interest. It became quieter, save for the constant, hoarse squawking of Mrs Pommerton's budgie. Mrs Pommerton raised her index finger and scolded in her distinctively shrill, high-pitched voice.

"Be quiet, Geronimo! Psst!"

Perhaps they would be privy to some juicy details about the recent goings-on at Parsley Manor. The butler commanded the attention of everyone in the room, and greeted them by nodding in acknowledgement. He walked to the counter with measured steps and waited for Simon to notice him.

Simon, however, was preoccupied with selecting index cards, while his back was turned to the butler. Mr Beanstock audibly cleared his throat to make his presence known.

Simon looked around and was taken aback for a moment.

"Mr Beanstock? What brings you here? I don't believe I have an index card for you, we'll have to issue one. Please take a seat. First of all, I must ask you to complete a questionnaire."

"I am not ill. To be more specific, I can attest to the fact that I haven't been ill since 1929 and have enjoyed optimum health since then, which I attribute to my healthy and balanced lifestyle."

"And what did you contract in 1929?" the nurse asked, slightly puzzled.

"Parotitis epidemica, a serious illness."

Low murmurs sounded among the waiting patients.

"How old were you then?"

"I was nearly 30 years old. It was very unpleasant."

"You suffered from mumps at the age of 30?" Simon Partridge asked a bit too loudly and incredulously.

151

Quiet giggles rippled among the patients.

"My dear Mr Partridge, such a disease isn't easy at that age. I was lucky to get away without any drastic repercussions."

Beanstock felt somewhat offended at the young man's impudent behaviour.

"Please excuse me", Simon murmured, "what can I do for you?"

"I urgently need to speak to both doctors. It won't take long."

"Just a moment, I'll ask if we can fit you in. You can see for yourself we're very busy today."

With these words, Simon emerged from behind the counter and disappeared into one of the treatment rooms.

Shortly afterwards, the door opened again and Dr Timothy Winterbottom carefully led a young lady out of the room. She was having problems getting through the door due to her conspicuously pregnant belly.

A young ruddy-complected man in the waiting room immediately leapt to his feet and rushed to the pregnant woman, who was now smiling contentedly.

"False alarm, Darling! I guess it will be a few more days – or weeks", the young woman explained.

"Weeks?" her husband exclaimed frantically. "You can't be serious, Doctor? I don't think I can get through this. Does this child even want to be born?"

Dr Winterbottom grinned.

"A baby arrives into the world when it wants to arrive. There's nothing I can do about it. Why don't you calm down. Besides, most babies are usually born at night. You can contact me at any time. Simon, the usual prescription."

Then he turned to Mr Beanstock.

"I have a full patient load today, can't it wait?"

"If you don't mind, I'd like to speak to you and your sister immediately. It will only take a few moments", the butler replied.

He turned to the patients who were waiting, "Please accept my apologies for the delay."

Murmurs of agreement signalled their collective response. The patients who were involuntarily kept waiting hoped to perhaps learn something interesting, since the doors were not very soundproof.

"Okay, Simon, I'll be right back. Please remove little Timi's bandage in the meantime." An anxious giggle was heard from the waiting room.

"Come, Mr Beanstock. Let's go next door to my sister's office."

Dr Rachel Winterbottom was sitting at her desk while writing down some notes on a card. Upon looking around she was surprised to see who her brother had brought into the office area.

"What's the matter, Mr Beanstock? Is something wrong with Junior?"

"No, Doctor, everything is fine with the animals at Parsley Manor. I've come to see you today for another reason. You must certainly know what has happened. I am trying to reconstruct the events on the day of the reception and would be very grateful if you could explain the nature of your disagreement with Miss Hillman. I noticed how both of you were upset after your conversation. Please help us clear up this tragic business."

"I must admit I find your request quite strange, Mr Beanstock. Unless I'm mistaken, isn't that the job of the police?" Dr Rachel wanted to know.

The butler could not help but notice the doctor sounded annoyed.

"There is no doubt that the police are very efficient, but Lady Fedora has already been considered as a suspect. And I will try my best to resolve the issue on behalf of the Baronets, which, in my opinion, includes Miss Hillman's background. Do you understand the gravity of the situation now, Doctor?"

"Why do you want to keep quiet after all this time, Rachel? Who would benefit from your silence? It certainly has nothing to do with the two deaths, so don't worry."

Dr Timothy Winterbottom soothingly put his hand on his sister's shoulder and nodded to her encouragingly.

She stood up and went to the window. After a moment she turned and nodded to her brother.

"A terrible matter, Mr Beanstock, I'm so sorry

about Bernice. Such a nice young girl. Timothy, please take over for me, I don't know if I'd be able to relive this."

"Well then, we went to school with Priscilla Hillman and her older sister Emely until they relocated to London. At that time, Sean O'Donoghue had just taken over the pub from his parents and expanded it. He was, no, he *is*, an attractive man and Rachel had been head over heels in love with him. Sean wasn't averse to my sister's infatuation, although of course our parents were to be kept in the dark. Rachel was still very young, after all. Only Sean and I knew about the forbidden romance, and regrettably Rachel's best friend, Priscilla's sister Emely, with whom I was very much in love. I always thought Emely was far prettier, and such a sweet person, a hundredfold kinder than her sister. Unfortunately, Emely likely thought nothing of it and mentioned the affair to her sister. Priscilla cold-heartedly pinched Sean from Rachel and to top it off, she betrayed her by telling our parents."

"Sean was only too pleased to be charmed by the lovely Priscilla and dropped me like an old sock. As a consequence, I was sent to a boarding school, which meant I was able to keep my parents from harassing Sean", Rachel continued. She paused for a moment.

"A short time afterwards, Priscilla became bored with her new toy and focused her attention on the Indian."

155

"Mr Divari, yes of course", Beanstock blurted out.

"Sean was terribly crushed. I think he actually loved Priscilla very much."

"But this is not an especially extraordinary story, if you excuse my frankness", the butler remarked. "Why were you so distraught on the day of the reception?"

The siblings looked at each other questioningly. Timothy Winterbottom gave a barely perceptible nod of encourage-ment. Rachel lowered her voice.

"Everybody knows that Sir Percival trusts you implicitly. Which is the reason I am sharing my juvenile impetuousness with you. Our parents are no longer alive. My mother, who had a staunch regard for Victorian etiquette, would have been horrified at my boldness. Fortunately, I am much more experienced than I was in those days and the relationship didn't work out. I tried to commit suicide at the boarding school. On the day of the reception I planned to confront Priscilla with this story but she was so arrogant. She laughed in my face and then told me in all seriousness that the affair with Sean had been a joke, and that it was solely for her own amusement. She told me I shouldn't be so histrionic. Do you understand now why I was so upset?"

"Oh, I understand much better now, and realise why the landlord was notably absent. I can also imagine why Mr Divari reacted so strangely. Many thanks for your candour. Thanks to my vocation as a butler, discretion is an integral component of my life philosophy."

Dr Timothy Winterbottom hugged his sister before he addressed the butler.

"If this statement could help the Baronets, it'd be worth it. Although I don't think it would avail you in any way. And if you were to ask us now whether we had an alibi? We had nothing to do with her death, believe it or not. And we're not holding a grudge. We truly feel sorry for her."

Beanstock bade the pair good-bye.

"Although I am not yet at liberty to make any comments, the truth lies somewhere in the past, of that I am sure. But I doubt your ghosts of the past are a part of it. Regardless, I am very grateful to you on behalf of the Baronets."

Beanstock left the surgery and instructed Gonzales to drive him to the pharmacy.

The only information Beanstock gleaned from the daughter of pharmacist Hoppleton was that Miss Hillman had deeply wounded her pride. Miss Hillman had not only described her appearance as tawdry and vulgar, but had also made it clear that she would never be successful in the movie industry due to her buzz saw voice. On his way out, Mrs Hoppleton whispered to him that her daughter had finally abandoned her dream of stardom in that den of iniquity known as Hollywood. The whole family was quite pleased – not to mention, relieved – about this decision.

Although wounded pride could be a strong motive for murder, Beanstock truly doubted Pamela would go to such extreme lengths. On the other hand, if the death was caused by poison, she would have been in the best position at the pharmacy to acquire it.

The butler considered making a stop at the pub, but then changed his mind. The chauffeur's initially hopeful grin was replaced by a resigned sigh.

He directed Gonzales to the golf hotel. Perhaps the next stop would yield more information.

The Bentley took a gentle turn in the driveway that led to the sparkling white *Rosebud* Hotel. Gonzales parked the car and stepped out of it along with the butler. The chauffeur retrieved a leather-bound cigar case from his jacket pocket and took pleasure in lighting up one of the slender dark brown beauties.

"I'll wait, Mr Beanstock, take your time", he mumbled with the cigar hanging from his mouth.

Beanstock was aware the chauffeur was already well-known all over town, even here at the hotel. While passing the wide entrance lined with columns he surmised that the ladies of Parsley Field simply couldn't resist his Spanish charm. Perhaps he could even benefit from this circumstance.

The entrance hall exuded dignified appeal. The entire ground level comprised a gleaming white marble floor. Several groupings containing a comfortable dark red plush sofa and dark red armchairs around a polished mahogany table each were placed on several small islands demarked by crimson Persian rugs. A spherical Art Deco lamp with multiple arms complemented each of the seating groups, and the hall corners were adorned with lush, fragrant rose arrangements in tall, ornate vases.

On the back wall, a double-wing multi-coloured glass door opened to the hotel restaurant. Tall glass doors granted an optimum view of the expansive golf course in the glistening sunlight of the early day.

A wide mahogany counter which served as the reception desk had been installed on the left wall of the entrance hall. The keys to the hotel rooms hung on gold-plated hooks behind the counter where Beanstock was heading.

The lady at the reception desk was Mrs Partridge, the postman's wife, who worked at the hotel every day. She only noticed the butler's presence when he was standing right in front of her and discreetly cleared his throat.

She became briefly startled when she looked up from the papers she had been reading. Beanstock immediately noticed her tear-stained, reddish eyes and pale complexion.

"Good afternoon, Mrs Partridge. Are you alright? You look rather out of sorts, if I may say so."

Mrs Partridge was a petite woman with pleasant facial features and chestnut hair that fell in soft waves around her shoulders. She struck a remarkable resemblance to her daughter, Phillis.

"Mr Beanstock, what is the purpose of your visit? There's nothing wrong at the hotel. I'm just very upset about Priscilla's death. And, of course, I'm terribly worried about my Phillis since her maid is also dead."

"You were employed with the Hillmans at one time, weren't you, Mrs Partridge?"

"Yes, that's right. I previously worked for the Hillmans as a nanny. It was so glorious to spend time with their two girls. I resigned from the position when I got married."

She looked at the butler with open irritation. She likely wondered why the normally reticent Beanstock was suddenly asking so many questions.

"Please excuse my curiosity, but did you ever encounter the children again?"

"I stayed in contact with the children and also tried to help them after they had moved to their aunt's place following their parents' terrible accident."

Mrs Partridge nervously flicked through the papers on the counter.

"So, what can I do for you?" she asked the butler once more.

"May I ask you whether you ever met this sinister aunt? Lady Fedora also tried to contact her godchild back then and was very harshly rejected."

Beanstock regarded Mrs Partridge with interest.

The receptionist did not look up from her papers and contemplated the butler's question as though concocting a reply.

Beanstock was a bit taken aback at her hesitation.

"Well, I actually met her twice. The first time was in her flat in London and the other time at the hospital in Bedlam, where poor Emely was being treated and then sadly passed away. This aunt was a strange person. Quite different from her brother, Mr Hillman. Yes, that's how it was..." She paused and turned to the key rack, as though she had to urgently sort the keys.

"Emely Hillman died in Bedlam?" Beanstock asked in astonishment.

"Yes, just as I've told you. Is there anything else I can do for you?" she replied with her back to Beanstock.

"I'd like to speak to Mr Divari and his secretary, if possible."

Mrs Partridge nodded and picked up the telephone receiver next to her. She pressed one of the buttons, waited, wryly smiled at the butler and spun around as though the mere sight of Mr Beanstock was disturbing. A click then sounded from the receiver.

Mrs Partridge relayed the butler's request and hung up shortly after.

"You may see Mr Divari now. He will receive you in his office."

She raised her hand and snapped her fingers at one

of the visibly bored bellboys who were hanging about in a corner. A young man with a pimply complexion came running at once.

"Please take Mr Beanstock to Mr Divari's office."

The young man bowed slightly and gestured for the butler to follow him. Beanstock wanted to say goodbye to Mrs. Partridge, but she had already disappeared through one of the doors behind the counter.

"How strange", he thought, "she must really be horribly upset over Miss Hillman's death."

He followed the bellboy, who was dashing ahead of him like an excited terrier. They walked down a wide corridor, past the kitchen from where the tinny clanging of pots and pans could be heard. A high-pitched nasal voice with a French accent shouted orders across the room, accentuated by an insistent *"Vite, vite"* after each sentence.

The bellboy then knocked on one of the high doors on the left.

"Come in", a female voice answered.

The bellboy opened the door for the butler, bowed with a grin and held out his hand. Beanstock looked at him uncomprehendingly.

The secretary, Miss Summerset, had meanwhile risen from her desk chair and approached the butler with a lascivious smile on her dark red lips.

She wore a tight suit in the colour of freshly cut grass, matching green, dizzyingly high stilettos and a grass-green, glittering emerald barrette in her wavy light blonde hair. The bellboy forgot his request for a tip and stared at Miss Summerset with unabashed interest.

"Don't you have anything else to do? Well, do you? Thank you. You may leave now!"

Reddish spots appeared on the bellboy's otherwise pale cheeks. He bowed slightly and rushed off.

"Mr Beanstock, to what do we owe the honour of your visit?"

Beanstock cleared his throat.

"It's regarding the day of the reception, Miss Summerset. The Baronets Parsley have enlisted me to investigate a few details in order to help solve the two murders. Although this is undoubtedly the job of the police, the honour of our house is at stake. I'm sure you understand."

"I don't know what could have been so extraordinary about that day, but Mr Divari will be pleased to receive you."

Miss Summerset floated away. In any case, Beanstock had the impression she was floating, although this notion seemed totally incomprehensible to him because of her heels, which were at least ten centimetres high. He had to force himself to avert this gaze from the lady in order not to seem indecent.

After a short while, Miss Summerset appeared and asked him into the hotel owner's office with a welcoming gesture.

As was customary while managing his hotel, Mr Divari wore an elegant grey suit. The moment the butler entered, the hotel owner politely stood up from his desk and approached him with an outstretched hand.

"Mr Beanstock, how are Milady and Sir Percival? Have there been any new developments?"

With these words, he gestured towards the comfortable seating area next to the fireplace.

"Thank you for agreeing to meet me, Sir", Beanstock replied with a curt bow. "I regret to inform you that it now appears to have been a murder, especially since our housemaid Bernice was also killed. Based on the initial forensic report, Inspector Greenwood suspects it was most likely poison, although the type of poison is yet unknown."

Visibly shocked, the hotel owner covered his eyes with his hand. He was unmistakably pained by the butler's statements.

"Miss Summerset, please have some coffee served. You'll join me in a cup of coffee, Mr Beanstock, won't you?" he asked his counterpart.

Beanstock rose briefly, then immediately sat down again with a smile when he realised he was not here in his capacity as a butler and thus not obligated to bring the coffee.

"I want to help with the investigation, Mr Divari. That is why I am here today. My intent is to reconstruct the day of the reception since I believe it might get me closer to the truth. What was that particular day like for you? I'd be interested in your reconstruction of the events."

In the meantime, Miss Summerset had returned, and shortly afterwards a waiter arrived with aromatic coffee in a silver pot on a shimmering silver tray, pink china cups and a silver étagère offering various dainties.

Miss Summerset poured the coffee and asked the butler whether he would like milk or sugar; he took both and she handed him the cup with her splendid smile.

Mr Divari then asked her to also sit down.

The hotel owner leaned back in his armchair.

"Well, now how would I describe that day… To be honest, I had not planned to attend this reception at all. Too many bad memories, you know. But Miss Summerset persuaded me to go. I promised myself I wouldn't speak to Priscilla, but it didn't turn out as such. She approached me, smiling, which gave rise to the tenuous hope that she still cared for me."

The butler noticed a movement from the corner of his eye and caught Miss Summerset clenching her hands into fists.

Davinder Divari continued his account of the reception.

"Priscilla, who of course now wanted to be called Inga, asked me to go into the garden with her. In my euphoria I tried to convince her that I still had affectionate feelings for her and missed her very much. I had tried to contact her several times, but never received a reply. But I was terribly wrong about her intentions. She couldn't stop laughing when I revealed my feelings for her. She told me that the time we had spent together was in the past and that she had only wanted to have fun back then. I didn't understand the world any longer. Do you understand what I'm saying, Mr Beanstock? I truly loved her and wanted to spend my life with her. This relationship nearly led to an estrangement from my family at the time."

He fell silent, took his coffee cup, then stood up and looked out of the large window onto the golf course where the first players were already congregating.

Beanstock turned his gaze to Miss Summerset. He immediately observed that she was visibly quite concerned about her employer. Perhaps there was more to their workplace relationship...? Or was she the one whose feelings were not reciprocated in this case?

"If you don't mind, I would like to remark that I watched you, Miss Summerset, and you were quite agitated upon your return from the garden. Did you speak to Miss Hillman?"

She gave Mr Divari a brief look of concern.

"I confronted her, yes, and I don't feel badly at all for what happened to her, sorry."

Mr Divari turned away from the large window and looked at his secretary in bewilderment.

"What did you say?" he wanted to know.

She hesitated and suddenly seemed to feel very uncomfortable. Beanstock noticed her face had taken on a grey pallor.

"Mr Divari, I told her in no uncertain terms that you are far too good for her. I told her to go back to Hollywood for good and have fun with the men over there. I immediately saw through her, that snake in the grass. Anything she did was to her own advantage and she relished in toying with other people's feelings. It's exactly how she behaved all her life. Even as a child she was terribly conceited. She was such a ..." She did not complete the sentence, lest she blurt out something inappropriate.

Beanstock raised his eyebrows in amazement. Someone was very much in love with her employer. He had caught on to it more quickly than the object of her desire. Mr Divari scrutinised his secretary as if noticing her for the first time in his life.

"If you decide to dismiss me now, then so be it; I can't change what I did or said. I simply could not bear the torment any longer. For you to put this slatternly tart on such a high pedestal was a farce. You suffered miserably all those years whereas she didn't even spare so much as a thought about you."

Miss Summerset angrily stomped out of the room.

Davinder Divari was still at a loss for words.

Beanstock finished his coffee and quickly stood up.

"Well, Mr Divari, I think this is fortunately quite a different scenario than involvement in the murder of Miss Hillman. I mean, you are very lucky, if I may say so, Mr Divari. I would like to bid you farewell and also thank you kindly for the information."

The hotel owner led him into the anteroom where Miss Summerset was busy clearing out her desk and tossing items into a small box.

"What are you doing, Miss Summerset?" Davinder Divari asked.

"There's nothing I can do if you send me away now. I understand." She added more quietly "I've always under-stood you."

Mr Divari ran to her, took her in his arms and held her for several minutes. So moved by his compassion, she could no longer blink back her tears that coursed down her made-up face.

Beanstock smiled.

"Alright then", he thought, "Seems I must have unwittingly set a romance in motion with all of my questions. Wonderful, just wonderful."

Ever the consummate gentleman and butler, he once again retrieved one of his pristine white handkerchiefs and handed it to Miss Summerset with a politely averted gaze.

"I must remember to order new handkerchiefs", Beanstock muttered to himself and made a note in a corner of his memory palace. He quietly retreated from the room, leaving the two lovebirds to sort things out on their own.

While crossing the hall towards the exit, he briefly glanced at Mrs Partridge to say goodbye. But the receptionist immediately averted her gaze and disappeared in the back room. Beanstock also made a mental note of this behaviour.

Upon the butler's arrival at the Bentley, Gonzales was nowhere to be seen – although the sound of giggling could be heard from the bushes beside the entrance.

When Mr Beanstock coughed a bit more loudly, two heads immediately appeared from behind the corner of the hotel.

Gonzales smiled at a cute little chambermaid who fixed her tousled hair and quickly disappeared with a curtsy.

"Señor Beanstock?"

"Gonzales?"

"How did it go, Señor?"

"I am satisfied with the outcome. Please take us home, Gonzales."

When Gonzales realised that the butler would not share any further information, he started the engine.

"*Maldito*", he mumbled, and loudly struck up a Spanish song, much to Beanstock's astonishment.

"Sing, Señor, it will calm your nerves. Come on!"

The butler looked at the happily warbling man beside him in puzzlement. Most enviable. Despite the tragedies around him, this man could still sing and be content. Beanstock retrieved his black notebook from his jacket pocket and wrote down the morning's findings.

"Ay, ay, ay, ay, ay mi morena de mi Corazón", Gonzales belted out to the residents of Parsley Field from his open car window while driving through the small town.

Sean was standing on a ladder outside his pub, thoroughly cleaning the new green sign bearing the gold inscription, *Jack O'Lantern*. He turned to his friend Gonzales and grinned with pleasure.

Old Mrs Pommerton was just returning from the stores with a full basket. She shot up a few inches, visibly startled by the chauffeur's ear-splitting vocal stylings. Beanstock leaned out of the open car window and apologetically waved at her. Her piercingly high-pitched scolding was drowned out by the chauffeur's crooning.

When they reached the driveway of Parsley Manor, they noticed the Inspector's police car parked out front. Beanstock disembarked and Gonzales drove the car into the garage.

"I look forward to more detective work whenever you like, Senor Beanstock, *trae alegria, Maldito!*" he called after the butler.

Beanstock entered the salon where the Inspector was having a conversation with the Baronets. He greeted the group with a slight bow.

Lady Fedora immediately turned to the butler.

"Imagine this: the police suspects a highly concentrated poison called ricin. Have you ever heard that an extract from the castor-oil plant could be highly poisonous? How terrible, my poor little Priscilla and our Bernice, what a tragedy."

Sir Percival swallowed audibly as he contemplated his castor oil consumption over the past few days and immediately poured himself another whisky.

"Darling, the Inspector has informed you that castor oil is completely harmless", Milady explained to her husband.

"And naturally he would like us tell him whether we grow this plant in our garden. You may check for yourself to ascertain we don't have such a plant here, Inspector Greenwood. Beanstock, kindly accompany the Inspector to our gardener and convince him of the correctness of my statement."

Then she added more to herself, "An essay about toxic plants. Perhaps I should give this some consideration?"

Sir Percival again audibly swallowed, looked at Junior lying beside him, whispered something in his ear and disappeared with the small dog, who was happily wagging his tail in anticipation of an extended walk.

Beanstock accompanied Inspector Greenwood into the garden.

"I am curious, Sir", the butler turned to the policeman who walked silently beside him. "How did you discover that poison was the cause of death?"

"Our coroner, Dr Seeker, took samples from the lungs. When combined with a certain substance, existing poison produces a specific colour reaction. He was able to immediately rule out arsenic and strychnine since a detection method for them has been in place for decades."

"I don't understand how he so quickly came up with this ricin, of all things. I've never heard of it before. How is this poison extracted? I would imagine it's a very complex procedure. Doesn't it require expert knowledge? How do you detect it? Is a detection procedure available? If I may speak candidly, you have an intelligent man in London, Sir. You're certain the poison was definitely absorbed through the lungs? This seems quite improbable."

"You don't have any other questions, do you?" the Inspector remarked, slightly annoyed. "All right then, it's extracted from the seed coats of the castor-oil plant. That's about as much as I've been able to understand. I suppose it's rather complicated... And therein lies your answer. Not to mention, it must have been an expert with prior knowledge. In order to be effective as quickly as it was in the two deaths, this poison must have been either very highly concentrated or mixed with another substance. Ricin only develops its full effect after several days according to the doctor.

He was able to detect morphine, but in the case of our two young and healthy ladies, a sole dose of morphine might not have been fatal. Considering the condition of the lung tissues and their blood levels, he recalled an examination in which he was involved due to his expertise in toxicology. After the war, strange samples declared as ricin had been found in an old warehouse in London.

Subsequent investigations had revealed that the army had experimented with the substance during the war; the warehouse had simply been forgotten. The documents found clearly indicate a strong likelihood of considerably higher quantities of this substance. Then the issue had suddenly became top secret. You see what I mean? The MI6 confiscated all the documents at that time. But as you have already recognised, our coroner is one clever chap. He managed to salvage some of the documents for his own studies. There were also photographs of poisoned organs which were outright disgusting. But he loves this work. The condition of the lung tissues, the blood levels and ultimately the comparison with these photographs suggest ricin."

Beanstock was not yet satisfied.

"How will he prove it, Inspector? I'm sure it won't be an easy task. And I doubt a judge will accept this photographic comparison."

Inspector Greenwood rolled his eyes and stopped

walking.

"Mr Beanstock, be that as it may, you're running the risk of overstepping with such inquiries. You can be assured that despite these tragic incidents, I still hope to be considered a friend of the Baronets. Any other policeman would send you packing. It's not in your nature to keep your nose out of it, is it? You think I've not been wise to your interrogations?"

"I greatly appreciate your forthrightness, Sir. But you know I would go to the ends of the earth for my employers."

"Yes, of this I'm aware, which certainly speaks highly for you. And I'm only sharing this information with you because I trust you'll keep it to yourself. To be honest, there is currently no chemical method for detecting ricin in the body. The claim is based on our coroner's intuition and the old documents regarding the effects of this infernal substance. According to Dr Seeker, it would only be feasible for him to establish the ironclad connection to the murders and to provide substantiated proof that ricin killed the two ladies if he had a sample of the poison that was used. I trust our doctor and his intuition. To this end, if we find the killer, we might even be lucky to find a sample of the poison and will then have sufficient proof to win a trial in court."

In the meantime, they had arrived at the greenhouse where Beanstock called for the gardener. Mortecai was the first to appear. He sniffed at the stranger, deemed him uninteresting by his standards and headed towards the flower beds. There were things to do that solely pertained to the tomcat. The gardener emerged from the greenhouse with a rake in his hand and a straw hat on his head.

"What can I do for you, Gentlemen?" he asked cautiously.

"Do you have a castor-oil plant in your greenhouse, garden, or on your personal property? Are you perhaps aware of any such planting in the environs of Parsley Manor?"

Beanstock looked at the Inspector in amazement. This question was truly embarrassing for a simple-minded man such as the gardener.

"What?" the gardener asked, visibly frightened. The butler quickly picked up the reins while gardener Herringbone stood in front of him, his eyes wide and hands shaking.

"Well, Herringbone, is there a castor-oil plant growing in the Baronets' garden?"

"Nope", the gardener mumbled.

"Do you keep this type of plant in the greenhouse?"

"Nope."

"Do you know anyone who has such a plant?"

"Nope. It won't even grow here."

"Say what?" the Inspector now asked in surprise.

"Well, in our area you would have to plant it every year, which might work, but this plant only flourishes in the tropics where it would grow to a few metres high. I think it's a spurge that doesn't feel at home here. That's the way it is."

"But in a greenhouse?" Beanstock asked.

"This could work, but it's costly. I don't know anyone who's tried it in our vicinity. However..." He interrupted himself.

"However?" the Inspector prompted.

"However, you have to use special soil for spurge plants, which doesn't exist in our region."

Speechless, Beanstock and Inspector Greenwood looked at each other in astonishment. After the Inspector had thanked Herringbone, the two gentlemen returned slowly to the house, each lost in thought.

Herringbone leaned on his rake and watched them, shaking his head. Mortecai returned from his walk, ambled around Herringbone's legs, purred and then looked up at his feeder. The gardener bent down, stroked him with a smile and said, "These amateur gardeners, they just don't have a clue about plants, do they, my friend? Well, how about a bowl of milk?" Mortecai seemed to agree with the suggestion, all the more so since he had just noticed Junior, his favourite adversary in the garden.

He quickly ran ahead of the gardener into the greenhouse.

Inspector Greenwood was the first to interrupt the silence, muttering:

"It was merely one of my ideas. Just to see whether this particular plant exists here. I guess it wasn't such a good idea, after all."

"Not necessarily, Sir. If we can rule out that anyone here had ricin at his disposal, this poison — if it is indeed ricin — must originate elsewhere. In that case we don't have many options, do we, Sir? Have you been able to rule out the pharmacist? Our prime candidate would have to be familiar with such things, don't you agree?"

"At this moment, Constable Donegal is in the pharmacy with a search warrant and a few colleagues from London, along with the Winterbottoms, of course. Our forensic expert, Dr Seeker, is also on the premises. Constable Donegal will be supervising the process. I can't even bear the thought of his excessive note-taking. I'll have to peruse all of them today. But I just wanted to visit the Baronets in person and smooth the waters. Do you understand?"

At that moment the Inspector realised he was still talking to the butler. "Well, it's really none of your business, Mr Beanstock. You're driving me mad with all your questions. Once again, please mind your own business. If you notice anything, tell me and don't do anything on your own. You can appreciate how dangerous it is. I'm convinced that Bernice either died by accident or knew too much."

Beanstock nodded in agreement.

"I believe the deaths of the two ladies were caused

177

by their use of cigarettes. We were told their lungs were full of this poison. In this case the cigarette containing the poison was literally the nail in the coffin. How odd that they didn't even find a single cigarette butt on Bernice's body. The killer could have removed it. But why would he remove the butt from here?"

The butler stopped short and squinted his eyes. Something about the Inspector's musings had captured his attention. Where were Miss Hillman's cigarettes? They could only be in her room and would be considered evidence. In any case, the forensics had not left the crime scene with any cigarettes. The butler had kept a wary eye on them.

Since Inspector Greenwood had not noticed anything, Beanstock kept on talking.

"What still remains is the old warehouse inventory in London. Who do you think was responsible for this back then? If we could find out who handled the items, we may already know the murderer's name."

"You're quite an astute man, Beanstock, but I must kindly ask you to immediately stop using the terms *we* and *us* regarding this investigation", the Inspector muttered.

Mysterious Encounters

After lunch, peace and quiet again prevailed at Parsley Manor.

Mr Van Horten retired to the library to place some urgent phone calls. After a heated battle of words, the Inspector had spelled out to him in no uncertain terms that he was obligated to stay. Although he would be at liberty to consult with his lawyer, it would also be a non-issue for Inspector Greenwood to arrange a restraining order from the responsible judge to prevent the publisher from leaving the premises. Despite the fact that Mr Van Horten certainly could attempt to contest these conditions, the publisher ultimately agreed contritely – albeit angrily. Nevertheless, he could not be expected to remain in this dump much longer, since work was piling up for him at his publishing house.

Lady Fedora took the expression *dump* personally and didn't deign to even look at the publisher again. After the chaotic goings-on and discussions over the past few days, she had serious misgivings about this publishing house. Her husband genuinely agreed with her and advised her to take her business elsewhere. Since the contracts only applied to the current book the publisher had requested, a re-orientation was certainly no problem. She could depend on her husband and his advice; he had always provided excellent counsel.

Sir Percival had allowed Mr Van Horten to occupy his study for the next few days and promised to render his assistance.

The Inspector had already telephoned the Baronets the previous day to inform them that the bodies of the two victims had been released and could be buried. There were no objections from the Hillman family's solicitor, Mr Pridges, of the venerable law firm Pington, Pington & Pridges in London. Due to the complicated circumstances, the reading of the will would take more time. The family's assets in England were one thing, but overseas assets were also to be considered.

Since the Baronets' lawyer had taken care of all the documentation and authorisations, Lady Fedora was able to plan the funeral arrangements. It was such a pity that there were no relatives to be found for either Priscilla Hillman or poor Bernice. Reverend Wilson was expected to arrive in the afternoon. Both deceased women were to be buried in the Parsley Field cemetery; Priscilla would be laid to rest alongside her sister and parents.

After a brief midday respite, Milady reappeared in

the salon. Beanstock was occupied with the afternoon tea table setting. He had voluntarily undertaken this task for which Bernice had always been responsible. While Lady Fedora observed him, she was moved to tears and had to reach for her handkerchief.

"She was such a lovely, pretty girl. I miss Bernice, Beanstock."

The visibly concerned butler kept silent. Mrs Argyle appeared in the doorway, carrying an etagere with small pieces of cake and sumptuous cucumber sandwiches the vicar was so fond of. She placed it on the table and nodded to the butler.

"We have set the table here in the salon, Milady, since it looks like rain and the terrace would certainly not be a wise choice under the circumstances. Upon your permission, that is."

Lady Fedora nodded her approval.

"It is perhaps a bit premature, Milady, but we have to think about recruiting for Bernice's position. I am very sorry, but we urgently require a housemaid." The housekeeper had tried to mildly articulate the situation so as not to appear cold-hearted.

Lady Fedora took a deep breath before she could muster a reply.

"Of course, I understand, Mrs Argyle. Please take care of the necessary details."

"Thank you, Milady."

"By the way, Mrs Argyle, the room", she paused, "Priscilla's room. It would be prudent to pack up her clothes and personal belongings. I'd like to do that myself, assisted by Filomena."

"Certainly, Milady. I'll arrange for Filomena to assist you."

Beanstock had fulfilled his duties in the salon and wanted to go to the kitchen to check the dinner preparations. Above all, he wanted to ask Filomena to keep an eye out for the cigarettes in Miss Hillman's room, since it could now be accessed again. But Lady Fedora detained him.

"Beanstock, please go and see Mrs Bloom. She phoned us to let us know that the condolence cards have arrived."

"With pleasure, Milady."

And thus it came to pass that Gonzales chauffeured the butler to Parsley Field again that day.

"So where are you going to snoop around this time, Señor Beanstock?"

"First of all, Gonzales, we're going to Mrs Bloom's place and second of all, I'm not "snooping around". I entrust these matters to His Majesty's Secret Service. I'm simply making inquiries to solve a heinous crime. Alright, let's go!"

Gonzales grinned.

"*Diablito*, shall we sing again? It'll add to the excitement, just like in those old Señor Bogart movies."

"If you don't mind, I would rather forego the singing."

"*Lástima!* As you wish, but it'll be only be half the fun."

After Gonzales had engaged first gear, the Bentley shot towards the driveway. All of a sudden, the chauffeur unexpectedly braked. Eyes wide with disbelief, he stared into the rear-view mirror. The sudden movement caused Beanstock to slightly pitch forward and he now glared angrily at Gonzales. When he noticed that the chauffeur had seen something amiss in the mirror, he looked behind him. The gardener had appeared from the rear garden.

His face was flushed with anger, and he had a strong grip on a man. A camera dangled from the neck of the small, scrawny figure. The gardener wildly gesticulated with his rake and his heated ranting became clearly audible. Beanstock got out of the car.

"Mr Herringbone, what on earth is the matter?"

"Imagine, Mr Beanstock. This little nosy parker has trampled on my beautiful, flowering stocks. Caught him sneaking across the garden with his fancy camera while he tried to climb over the back patio railing. And in the process, he destroyed my..." he cleared his throat, "I mean, in the process, he destroyed Milady's flowers."

Beanstock took a closer look at the diminutive man who was trying to break free from the gardener's firm grip. His dirty and threadbare plaid brown suit was already long worse for the wear. His shoes were very filthy due to his activity in the garden and a button was missing from his jacket. The man did not wear a hat, which would have been appropriate considering the greasy, fuzzy shock of hair on his half-bald head. The butler noticed these features straightaway.

"I know you, don't I? Didn't I already eject you from the property a few days ago? There isn't anything more to see here and I demand respect for the privacy of the Baronets of Parsley. Should I catch you here again, I'll immediately report you to the police."

Herringbone reluctantly released the small man. The reporter adjusted his clothes and quickly found his voice.

"Hey, Mister, consider yourself lucky if I don't decide to sue you. This is my best suit and I'm just doing my job here. Inga Hillman was a Hollywood star and readers are eager to discover something sensational about her."

Gonzales had joined them in the meantime, grabbed the reporter's jacket by the lapel, and then pulled him up until they were at eye level. The man's legs dangled in the air and his complexion took on a shade of pale pink.

"*Ir al Infierno, Diablito*, otherwise I will personally show you the road to hell!" the furious Spaniard hissed directly into the self-important little man's face.

Then he let go of him and the reporter ran off without a backward glance. In the process, the film compartment of the camera magically opened and its film fluttered out like a garland.

Gonzales smiled mischievously.

"We won't be seeing him again", the gardener stated with satisfaction.

"Moscardón!" Gonzales called after him.

"What did you say?" the gardener asked.

"Well, what would be the word in your language…" Gonzales thought hard and a deep furrow appeared between his eyes, "for a buzzing, disgusting, green..."

"Blowfly!" the butler replied. He turned around and quickly walked back to the car, otherwise the other gentlemen would have noticed his satisfied facial expression. They looked at each other and smiled. Herringbone returned to his damaged stocks, whistling as he went, while Gonzales hummed a tune and then sat down in the driver's seat of the Bentley.

"Well done, Señor Gonzales", Beanstock mumbled.

Gonzales, who had never been addressed as Señor by the butler, knew he had done a very good job and grinned from ear to ear as he drove towards Parsley Field. Beanstock asked the chauffeur to stop at the pub.

"Wait for me at Mr O'Donoghue's." He winked at him knowingly.

Gonzales smiled at the prospect of a proper drink with his friend, Sean, After all, they still hadn't made a toast to the beautiful new sign above the entrance. He disappeared into the pub, rubbing his hands in anticipation. He was fully aware that such a rare moment in which he was allowed to go to a pub with the approval of Parsley Manor's respectable butler would not happen again in the near future.

In the meantime, Beanstock took a shortcut to Mrs Bloom's shop and climbed the two steps up to the door.

Mrs Bloom was busily walking back and forth between a huge cardboard box and a tall white shelf. New glass jars kept emerging in all shapes and sizes: big, small, thick, thin, curved as well as globular candy jars with a thick lid on top. Some of them had already been filled with sweet confections and the white-haired lady beamed with joy at the sight. Beads of perspiration were forming on her forehead. A pair of scissors dangled from a red thread she had attached to her pink apron, which she used to adroitly open the bags from another box, filled with England's most popular sweets. She sliced open the bags and released the contents into the jars and then carefully lifted the candy-filled jars to their designated place on the shelf. Afterwards she put a label adorned with fine penmanship on each jar. Beanstock watched for awhile as she carried her meticulous process to fruition, rapt with fascination.

"Mrs Bloom, what kind of confections do you have there?" he finally asked to storekeeper.

The old lady rose and only now realised she had a customer.

"Oh, Mr Beanstock, I apologise. I was so absorbed in my work. Just look!"

With rosy cheeks and eyes widened with pride, Mrs Bloom described her new acquisition.

"Wine gums, fruit gums, caramel cream fudge and toffees, white as well as green peppermints, candies in all sumptuous flavours, my latest offerings. My word, they've finally arrived. I've been impatiently waiting for weeks for Mr Partridge to pay me a visit during his rounds. Well, I suppose these things take time nowadays. Sir Percival had given me the address of the supplier in London, as you already know.

In these times of sugar rationing, it's a veritable miracle. And these wonderful jars. Custom-made, Mr Beanstock! Fine English craftsmanship."

During her last words, she had defiantly crossed her arms and furtively glanced toward the pharmacy. The butler was aware of the bitter rivalry between Mrs. Bloom and Mrs. Hoppleton.

Upon a closer look at the jars, Beanstock spotted an inconspicuous embossed stamp bearing the inscription: *Made in Italy*.

Mrs Bloom immediately turned the jar around.

"As I was saying, fine English craftsmanship!"

Beanstock cleared his throat.

"Very nice, Mrs Bloom, no doubt, they'll become very popular in and around these parts. Lady Fedora ordered condolence cards which I'd like to collect now, if it's not too much trouble."

"Just a moment, please. I'll fetch the cards straightaway." She disappeared into the back room for a short while and returned, opening the small box she held in her hand.

"How beautiful these cards are. I had them printed in the same shop which also printed the invitations for the reception. The printing company is known for its excellent, traditional English craftsmanship. Just how we prefer it out here. I suppose you simply forgot some of the invitations for the reception back then, am I right, Mr Beanstock? By the way, a book has also arrived for you."

With these words, she again disappeared to the back room, leaving a perplexed butler in her wake. He could not fathom what she might have meant by the forgotten invitations. When she returned and placed the book on the counter, he immediately inquired what she meant by her comment.

"I was referring to the Partridges. What makes you ask? When I noticed that Mrs Partridge was very distressed and had run out of the garden on the day of the reception, I thought they might have forgotten to send her the invitation which was the reason she left in such a huff. I didn't see our postman there, either. Well, I would have considered it odd if the Baronets had invited the postman. No offense, Mr Beanstock. Nobody wants a commotion in the village. We keep things behind closed doors, isn't that right? It's nobody's business if the Baronets deem it acceptable to consort with folks below their station."

The butler's eyebrows shot up. He wasn't sure if Colonel Bloom's widow was aware she didn't belong to either social class.

Beanstock gave some thought to Mrs Bloom's version of events which prompted him to recall Mrs Partridge's strange behaviour at the hotel. To be sure, it might have been on account of her having been the Hillman children's nanny and simply wanting to see her girl. But why had she run away in such an upset state? Had she spoken to Miss Hillman? No one had noticed anything of the sort.

But perhaps something quite different had upset her so. What if she had recognised Mr Van Horten? He now felt a strong urge to speak to this gentleman.

He wondered whether it was advisable to share his suspicions with the Inspector, but felt it would be too premature at this juncture since he lacked any substantive evidence. Nor did he intend to embarrass Mrs Argyle.

Beanstock counted the exact amount of money for his purchase, placed it on the counter, and said goodbye to Mrs Bloom. She was already preoccupied with her candy world again, filling the jars with lemon drops.

He walked to the pub, lost in thought.

Upon his return to Parsley Manor, he handed the condolence cards to Lady Fedora.

"They are utterly beautiful, Beanstock", she whispered.

"Oh, one more thing, we've packed Priscilla's suitcases. Please instruct Harrison to store them in the laundry room upstairs until further notice. We don't know what to do with them yet. Until then, let us wait for the reading of the will."

"Anything else, Milady?" the butler asked with a respectful bow.

"Just one more thing... have you found Priscilla's golden cigarette case anywhere? It wasn't in her room."

"So, the cigarette case has disappeared?" the butler mused as if to himself. „That's interesting. No, I haven't seen it."

This was the puzzle piece Beanstock had been missing. Since he had learned the method of the poisoning, he had suspected the cigarettes to be the catalyst of the deadly poison. But where had they gone? He would have liked to search Van Horten's room, but how could he even go about it? While there were only two possibilities for the whereabouts of the cigarette case, Beanstock's gut feeling, told him that only one of them would yield results.

"Bernice, you stupid girl, what have you done", he muttered softly.

The funeral took place on a rainy Saturday. Rain and funerals had been part and parcel for generations. The day seemed to pass in slow motion.

The black veil over Lady Fedora's hat fluttered in the wind like a dark, fateful cloud of mist. A steady procession of open black umbrellas approached the church at Parsley Field where a white coffin had been placed, surrounded by an abundance of white roses.

A collective decision with Reverend Wilson had been made to bury Inga Hillman in the morning and Bernice in the afternoon; a joint funeral service would have seemed inappropriate. Although the fateful day was already twice as onerous for those involved, Lady Fedora had insisted on it and Reverend Wilson had not challenged her decision.

The Baronets and Mr Van Horten sat in the front row of the church, while the inhabitants of Parsley Field were relegated to the pews behind them. A small group of journalists had been allowed to attend.

A representative of Inga's acting agency in Hollywood and a member of the film studio in London were also in attendance. A black Rolls Royce turned heads when it arrived shortly prior to the ceremony. A gentleman attired in a black coat with a slouch hat pulled low over his face disembarked from the vehicle and sat down in the rear pew near the exit.

A murmur sounded through the small row of journalists; it was rumoured that the gentleman was a renowned actor. At the same time, a sexton brought in a lavish grave decoration consisting of at least a hundred red roses and placed it by the coffin. *To my beloved Inga from E. F.* had been written in golden letters on the black ribbon. When the coffin was carried outside at the end of the ceremony, the enigmatic gentleman had already disappeared.

Beanstock had chosen a seat in the church next to the columns where he had an optimum view of the mourners. Inspector Greenwood joined him with his Constable and asked if Beanstock was likewise keeping an eye out for the murderer.

The ceremony proceeded according to protocol. When the mourners made their way to the gravesite, the butler observed something that captured his attention: Mr Van Horten had remained in the church. Beanstock tried to keep an eye on the entrance, and within five minutes Mr Van Horten suddenly rushed out and ran away as if possessed by the devil.

Beanstock might have been able to witness more, but his attention was deflected at that moment by Lady Fedora who nearly collapsed under the weight of the tragic incidences. He approached Sir Percival to offer his assistance. If he hadn't been distracted, he would have noticed another individual leaving the church who gazed after the publisher with a mischievous grin.

The funeral service for beautiful Bernice proceeded slightly differently. An exquisite white coffin was also placed in front of the altar adorned with fragrant white lilacs on top which had been arranged by Mr Herringbone personally. The priest bade farewell to the young girl with words just as perfectly articulated as those for Inga Hillman. Contrary to the morning service, there was nobody else at the ceremony aside from the Baronets Parsley, accompanied by their servants in the first pew.

The gravesite in the corner of the cemetery consisted of a plain white tombstone bearing the inscription: *Bernice Bernstein, we will not forget you.*

Her year of birth and death had been engraved next to the epitaph. None of her relatives who might have wanted to express their sympathy had been tracked down. In this instance, it was primarily Filomena Arbuckle who required moral support. She was likely the one who had known Bernice best.

This tragic day would be etched in the memories of the inhabitants of the small village, particularly the inhabitants of Parsley Manor. Any interested parties in the Commonwealth as a whole now knew the location of Parsley Field, though its sudden notoriety was not welcome. Unfortunately, its pseudo-celebrity status also attracted many curious strangers to the town in the days following the widely publicised tragedy, but they were only interested in the macabre tale of the film star and did not spend a single pound in the village. Although Mr Templar's station experienced a distinct upsurge of visitors, it was quite the opposite at landlord Sean's *Jack O'Lantern*. And Reverend Wilson had his hands full with all the trampled lawns surrounding the Hillman family grave.

But as is the case for sensational news anywhere in the world, this one would be forgotten and replaced by a new scandal. The name "Inga Hillman" might only be mentioned in passing in a year's time, but after another year the Hollywood beauty would be an afterthought. Her name would be relegated to documentaries or biographies. Authors would exploit her memoirs to augment sales of their books, and directors would dedicate films to Inga in order to reap profits with the tragic story.

But by then the world would have found a new beautiful starlet worth worshipping.

Old Houses – Old Stories

Silence prevailed at Parsley Manor as the residents entered the mansion. Mrs Porkpie had prepared some refreshments for the servants in the kitchen.

The staff gathered together and told stories.

"Do you remember the day when Bernice came to us? She was such a nervous little thing", Mrs Argyle smiled serenely at the memory. "And she had no belongings, save for a small suitcase and her references. I hired her on the spot and she turned out to be an asset for our mansion, wouldn't you agree, Mr Beanstock?"

"Indeed, she was. We shall all miss her."

"Do you remember the incident involving the fireplace in the salon?" the cook asked, smiling. A collective grin confirmed their unanimous response.

"She had forgotten the chimney sweep was still on the roof and wanted to light a fire. She had just put her head into the chimney to properly stack up the firewood, when she became enveloped by a cloud of soot from above. I believe she was still coughing the next day. Lady Fedora sent out for some chest compresses. Bernice's dress was utterly ruined and her feet left black traces all over the entire house."

Mrs Porkpie wiped a tear from her eye. Phillis set a delectable ring cake on the table and cut it into pieces.

"This was the cake she liked best", she explained quietly to those present. "How very sad that we were the only friends she had. Was there truly nobody else to be found, Mr Beanstock?"

"Milady has made a valiant effort to obtain details from her solicitor. And Mrs Argyle wrote to the vicar of the town where she had been baptised. Unfortunately, there only seemed to be the one aunt who passed away years ago."

The butler stood up, nodded to the group and went into the salon. The Baronets sat solemnly with their tea. Junior had slipped quietly under the table and seemed to instinctively sense the depressed atmosphere in the room. The publisher's place setting remained untouched.

"Is there anything else I can do for you, Sir, Milady?" the butler asked.

"You may clear the table. And if you would be so kind as to bring me a whiskey, Beanstock", Sir Percival replied.

Beanstock turned to his employer inquiringly.

"May I ask the whereabouts of Mr Van Horten? I

need to speak to him urgently."

It had evidently escaped Lady Fedora's notice that the publisher was absent at tea time. "Perhaps he's gone for a walk. The weather is better now. It just occurred to me that I haven't seen him since Priscilla's funeral, to be honest. Where might he be, Darling?" she asked her husband beseechingly

The Baronet shrugged his shoulders.

"At any rate, he's not in the library. I was just there to get a book and he wasn't anywhere to be found. What peculiar behaviour, I must say! Guest don't usually just come and go as they please. Such unseemly behaviour! I strongly advise you to change publishers, my girl. Even our manservant has better manners."

The Baronet had reverted to his tendency to pontificate, but then managed to control himself. Beanstock took the tray into the kitchen. After serving whiskey to the Baronets, he accompanied Gonzales to the garage. He was curious whether the publisher's car was still parked there, since he could have easily slipped away while everyone else was preoccupied with the funerals. Beanstock had a specific question to ask him and had been waiting for days for an opportune moment to confront him accordingly, but the publisher always seemed to be indisposed.

Gonzales opened the garage where the Atalante had been parked. It was still in the same place as on the first day.

Beanstock returned to the kitchen where the table had already been cleared, and evening dinner was being prepared.

Mrs Argyle had received the first batch of applications for the housemaid position upon enlisting an agency in London.

Now she was waiting for the butler to review them; she was obligated to include him in the selection of manor personnel.

"Does anyone know the whereabouts of the publisher Mr Van Horten? Has anyone seen him leave the mansion?" the butler asked his colleagues.

At first no one responded, but then Mrs Argyle spoke up.

"Well, he's not in his room. I had Harrison clean the fireplace half an hour ago. Perhaps he's working in the library?"

"No, and his car is still in the garage. Milady assumed he might have gone for a walk."

Beanstock was not convinced. He recognised the pressing need to search Van Horten's room and was loath to wait any longer. Could he possibly get away with committing such an indiscretion? The telephone rang, which startled Filomena Arbuckle and caused her to shriek. Phillis turned pale and Mrs Porkpie dropped her spoon into the soup. The nerves of everyone in the room were on edge after the series of tragic events.

Since he was certain that Milady and Sir Percival had retired for the evening, Beanstock went to the telephone on the kitchen wall and answered it.

"Parsley Manor, Mr Beanstock speaking, how may I help you?"

"*Daisy-chain!*" a soft voice replied on the other end of the phone.

Beanstock beamed from ear to ear. His left hand automatically grasped the lapel of his jacket and reached for the round pin. The tiny, unobtrusive daisy was scarcely visible. Beanstock was the only one in Parsley Manor who knew the significance of this little gem.

In the meantime, something quite unusual was taking place a few kilometres away. The foreboding old Hillman house loomed in front of Mr Van Horten like an unsurmountable menace. Although he could easily have taken his vehicle, it seemed too unsafe to him; he might have been watched. As a consequence, he had opted instead to navigate the fields on foot and was now peering down at his dirty, custom-made shoes with great displeasure. A deep crease of anger formed between his eyebrows. The muddy particles had ruined the fine leather.

He retrieved a fine handkerchief from his pocket and tried to remove the mud. Would he ever be able to get away from this horrible place? What did they have on him, anyway? There wasn't actually anything specific. Or any means to prove it. This extraordinary poison was his creation. But why was he even here in the first place? He was hard-pressed to reconcile his own actions.

The fear of losing his hard-earned status all but consumed him. After so many years he believed he was finally safe. And now someone who knew his secret had suddenly appeared and was threatening him. He had easily disposed of the little blackmailer. In a way, she had brought about her own demise. He smiled at the thought. Van Horten reached into his jacket pocket and felt the cold metal of his revolver.

Dark clouds chased across the sky. If it started to rain again his suit would surely also be ruined. He looked up at the dark façade of the house which had been erected in an austere, classical style.

A triangular gable with implied columns from the roof to the floor towered above the entrance portal. The tall windows were adorned with floral garlands made from grey stone. Many of these accoutrements were unfinished or in a state of disrepair, and the tall windows were dark.

What had once been a beautiful country house with a flourishing English garden had since succumbed to decay and lifelessness. Old leaves and withered plants were piled up everywhere. There was a rustling in the tall grass while the four-legged visitors had long since appropriated the old walls and had made themselves at home in dark crevices and beneath the old cupboards.

Van Horten ascended the stairs to the entrance. The door was slightly ajar, and when he pushed it fully open, the creaking of the tall wooden door seemed to reverberate up to the top floor and make its echoing return.

The furnishings were visible even in the sparse light. Chesterfields, tables and cupboards were covered with white fabric that had become sullied with dust over the decades. A faint light seemed to emanate from the top floor. Van Horten approached the wide staircase and listened for any sounds above him, but was greeted by silence. He cautiously made his way upstairs, step by step. The light originated from a room on the first floor.

"I'm here now, just as we agreed. Let's just get this over with!" Van Horten shouted upwards. His voice sounded unnaturally loud and echoed amid the silence.

He then pushed open the door to the room and gripped his revolver even more tightly.

Aside from a round mahogany table situated in the centre, the room seemed empty. The wood was gleaming as though it had just been polished by a fastidious maid. A candelabra holding a lone candle was placed on the table, illuminating a dim pool of light around it.

Van Horten noticed something next to the table that elicited a smile from him. He unclasped the revolver and removed his hand from his jacket pocket in order to retrieve it.

When he touched the object of interest, he felt a slight sting. Startled, he recoiled as he withdrew his hand and saw a small drop of blood on his finger.

"Doctor Richard McLean, we finally meet again. Let's have a little chat, shall we?"

All of a sudden, the voice sounded from the darkness of the room.

Van Horten's hand shot back to the revolver in his pocket.

"My name is Van Horten", the publisher hissed with contempt.

"Of course, I'm fully aware of the name you now use. Take a closer look at the items on the table. I already mentioned them in the church. Come on, don't be afraid. Take a close look at the little trinkets that a pretty, innocent young thing coveted as though they were precious treasures."

The publisher drew closer.

The items had been meticulously arranged on the table. At the centre next to the candelabra was a small wooden box with a partially faded dark red rose on its lid. A silk cloth had been spread out next to it as a makeshift tablecloth for the array of small items: a rusty key, a wide black velvet ribbon, a faded cinema ticket and a cheap-looking pink ring. Next to these objects was the very item Van Horten had been searching for: Priscilla Hillman's golden cigarette case. It was open, revealing three untouched cigarettes and one cigarette butt inside. The filigree writing inside the lid was gleaming, and the vanilla scent of *Shalimar* hung in the air like a bad omen.

"Did you know I was there that day, Richard? I'm allowed to call you Richard, don't you think? Besides, we've known each other for such a long time, haven't we?"

"I don't know you and my name is *not* Richard", Van Horten spluttered, wiping his sweaty brow with his hand. He started to feel dizzy at this farcical situation. All he really wanted was to grab the case and immediately abscond with it.

"Richard, Richard, Richard. Are you not feeling well? What a poor host I am. Why don't you sit down."

The sound of a squeaking armchair emerged from one of the dark corners towards the publisher. The red plush chair with a gold pattern settled at the edge of the table.

"Isn't this armchair beautiful? In my mind's eye I can envision little Priscilla sitting in it while playing with her dolls. You can see it too, can't you, Richard? Oh no, belay that! It's her sister Emely that you're seeing, isn't that right? You certainly had your way with her in Bedlam back then, didn't you?"

Van Horten had clumsily plunked down in the armchair. He didn't understand what was happening to him. Why was he so dizzy? The faint stinging sensation came to mind and he looked at his finger. The drop of blood had disappeared while the puncture site had turned a slight blue. He had previously been a physician and knew exactly what these symptoms meant.

But his mind was no longer functioning properly. He quickly glanced at the cigarette case. There was a tiny, practically invisible needle affixed to its side. "I truly owe you an apology. One little needle prick and suddenly you have given me your undivided attention, am I correct? It could not be otherwise. Hmmm, what else was I compelled to tell you before you are gone forever…?"

Steps could be heard in the darkness. Somebody was pacing around the room.

"Ah well, I was also at the manor on those festive evenings. I desperately wanted to see her. Priscilla was quite pretty, don't you agree? She almost caught me spying under her window, but I managed to get away undetected. Why were you so afraid? Her death was absolutely pointless. Although she recognised you, she would have returned to her fanciful world and you could have continued leading your meaningless life. And then there was pretty little Bernice. Tsk, tsk, tsk! Richard, what you did was truly evil. You deliberately accepted the possibility of her death. Perhaps you were even the one who gave her a light for her first cigarette that evening. I saw her, but it was too late by then. Which is the reason her treasures are here for us to enjoy."

Van Horten could not move a muscle. He only had the capacity to listen. He had injected this particular drug into his patients whenever they did not comply with his demands. Thus it was futile to reach for the revolver. He knew the exact side effects of the drug coursing through his veins.

A slender hand reached out of the darkness for the wooden box and returned the objects that had meant so much to Bernice. Van Horten watched the action with increasing terror. The box disappeared from his field of vision. Rasping softly, he whispered something towards his invisible host. A shadow appeared next to his mouth. Someone was leaning over him.

"Is there anything else you'd like to tell me?"

Small, dirty streaks of sweat were now trickling down Dr Richard McLean's face. The shadow whispered something in his ear with a mischievous smile on his lips. A slender hand was placed on his shoulder and clenched it, before it disappeared again from his field of vision.

"And of course you couldn't keep that to yourself, could you?" the voice whispered out of the darkness. Moments later, a rope with an elaborately knotted noose darted out onto the table, similar to those used by the hangmen of London. A slight spasm ran through the publisher's body.

"You see, Dr Richard McLean, Doctor of

Psychiatry and graduate of the famous Cambridge University, this rope signals the demise of a murderer. You should not have come to Parsley Manor, my friend. I've been looking for you for a very long time. I would likely have never found you had you not come to me. Please give my regards to Emely's and Priscilla's Aunt Agatha when you get to Hell. You must surely know each other, no? As I've heard, you got along famously with that horrible old lady."

The candle extinguished.

Everything grew pitch dark around Dr McLean.

"Agatha Christie, the great lady of crime fiction, once aptly stated 'old sins cast long shadows'. Let us now see how long your shadow will be when you hang."

Daisy-Chain

"*Daisy-Chain*", Beanstock uttered in response to the caller's words.

After a brief pause, a calm voice answered at the other end.

"Black speaking, our representative at Bethlehem Royal Hospital was successful. He found some enlightening documents, and a copy of them is already on its way to you. As always, I trust we were able to help. *Daisy-Chain*, Mr Beanstock."

"*Daisy-Chain*, Mr Black." Beanstock slowly returned the receiver to its cradle. He contemplated the situation at hand. It had indeed been proper to investigate at the hospital after listening to Mrs Argyle's story and upon discovering Emely Hillman's death had occurred at that particular clinic.

It was fortunate that a community bound by integrity still existed. He smiled at the history of it. In the 19th century, working conditions for servants had been difficult. Their days were lengthy, and any days off were few and far between. Duties for the maids and servants were physically taxing and all too often claimed their victims through illness and death.

A butler from the venerable household of Lord Clarky of the Ginger Heights founded a community which was dedicated to improving and upholding the rights of service staff. At that time, what was solely a relief organisation very quickly transformed into a conspiratorial group that spread like an invisible network throughout Great Britain. At that time the name *Daisy-Chain* came into existence. The group operated covertly in the same way as an inconspicuous daisy wreath that had become an extensive, labyrinthine chain. The tiny button with the delicate flower was the identification mark among the members. Whenever a member needed help, the rest were immediately and efficiently at their disposal without leaving a trace.

All that was required was a phone call or a letter containing the code word. There were special contacts for every location in Great Britain. And there were precious few injustices that could not be exposed. Servants were secretive by nature and a proper servant was unconditionally loyal to his employer. Be that as it may, they often heard and saw things that were not intended for public consumption, and it was not rare for them to know more than the police on a frequent basis. Thus the simple relief organisation had become a community which was even better organised than His Majesty's spies. There were secret meetings in the cities and even a large annual gathering for the upper echelons in the *Daisy-Chain* network.

Beanstock had not engaged the services of the community very often in the past. But in this case, the effort seemed justifiable: light had to be shed on the impregnable darkness.

Mrs Argyle quietly cleared her throat behind his back.

"Could we have a brief discussion regarding the applications, Mr Beanstock?"

"Yes, of course. Why don't we meet in my office."

It took an entire hour to select three suitable applicants from the pile. The London agency had offered several recommendations. Shortly after the war, many young girls sought respectable employment which was often scarce in the cities. For most of them, there was little else save for factory work. Landing a job at Parsley Manor was highly desirable for a trained maid since it was known in service staff circles that its employees could anticipate excellent working conditions. And the wages were also quite decent. Mrs Argyle would inform the agency that the three candidates should come for the interview in the next few days, at which time they would make a decision.

The butler had also made a decision. He walked quietly into the hall and made his way upstairs to the bedrooms where he stopped and listened. He was met with complete silence.

Beanstock headed toward the guest rooms and entered the room Van Horten currently occupied. It was not only the Baronets who would be relieved once he finally left.

Beanstock surveyed the room. It looked tidy. He suspected Mrs Argyle was personally tending to its upkeep at the moment.

The publisher had travelled light. There was only one suitcase next to the wardrobe. Beanstock grabbed it and opened it on the floor. It was empty.

The bespoke suit from the reception, a casual jacket and a few light-coloured shirts hung in the wardrobe. A pair of bench made black patent leather shoes sat on the floor beneath the garments. Beanstock quietly closed the wardrobe. The chest of drawers in the far left corner was empty except for socks and undergarments. In the small bathroom, he found only a few toiletry articles, a bottle of cologne, a razor together with a soap dish and brush as well as a hairbrush.

It then occurred to him that the publisher always carried a black briefcase. He looked around for it and eventually found it under the bed. Its contents predictably comprised files and letters, but nothing personal. Disappointed, he put the briefcase back under the bed when something caught his attention.

Beanstock noticed an object under the chest of drawers in the corner, a very tiny, oblong piece of cloth or leather. Although he could scarcely identify it, he immediately recognised it as out of place. He carefully moved the piece of furniture forward and bent down against the wall. Someone had ostensibly tried to plant it on the narrow ledge along the back wall. It looked like a flat, dark leather case, and in all likelihood had slipped on its side, which had brought the black leather flap to the butler's attention; he would never have otherwise discovered it had he not looked under the bed.

Beanstock retrieved the white gloves he always carried with him from his jacket. After all, silverware was to be polished, paintings carefully removed, or the Baronet's garments had to be set out. One ought not to leave fingerprints anywhere on the lordship's treasures, a cardinal rule taught at every estimable butler's school.

He hastily donned his gloves and proceeded to dislodge the object: an oblong case with a zipper. When he opened it, his face took on a knowing expression. Aside from a few sachets of white powder, comparable to the ones the police had found on Miss Hillman's person, the case contained two syringes and several small glass vials filled with coloured liquids.

The sound of footsteps was heard in the corridor in front of the room. Beanstock retrieved one of the yellow-tinged vials, shut the case and then put it back where he had found it. This liquid might perhaps be the poison sample needed by Dr Seeker and thus provide concrete evidence.

He quickly went to the door and leaned his ear against it. Had Mr Van Horten just returned? How would he be able to explain his presence in his room? As fast as lightning, he conjured up an excuse when the door handle moved slowly and then carefully swung open.

"Mr Beanstock?" a startled voice yelled.

Beanstock sighed with relief.

"Harrison, what's the matter?"

The servant entered the room with a bucket and a plunger, every plumber's indispensable little helper.

"Mrs Argyle asked me to see what was wrong with the toilet. She claims it might be clogged. But I can come back later..."

The butler interrupted him.

"The toilet bowl? Hmmm. No, no need to come back later, just follow your orders. In fact, I'll join you. Let's go see what's wrong with it."

The servant looked at him with open astonishment.

Mr Beanstock the butler was actually offering to help him fix a toilet? Harrison shrugged and went into the bathroom next door. He had already experienced much stranger things in this household.

Beanstock opened the toilet bowl lid and pulled the chain. A gurgling sound was heard before the bowl filled up with water.

"It is, in fact, not flushing properly. You can take it

from here, Harrison", the butler said.

Harrison scratched his head nervously. He retrieved the plunger from the bucket and began to pump, which took a while. Beads of sweat formed on the servant's brow. After several minutes, strange tubular-shaped objects emerged. "What's that?" Harrison marvelled, and the two gentlemen bent over the toilet bowl. Small, narrow tubes with thin, brownish fibres were bobbing up and down in the gurgling water. Beanstock grabbed Harrison's plunger, turned it upside down, and fished out some of the tubes using the wooden handle. The two gentlemen looked at each other.

"Looks like tobacco, Mr Beanstock."

"Exactly, Harrison. It *is* tobacco and these tubes that are now drenched were originally cigarettes. Quite a lot of them must have been dumped to actually clog the toilet. My guess is a whole pack."

"But if the man doesn't want to smoke, why doesn't he just toss them into the wastepaper basket? I don't get it."

Harrison scratched his head again absentmindedly.

"Well, the most important aspect here is that Mr Van Horten doesn't even smoke. Harrison, just leave the toilet as it is."

The servant was now utterly confused. "But the gentleman can't possibly use it in this condition, Mr Beanstock, and Mrs Argyle specifically gave me instructions to…"

Beanstock interrupted him again.

"It's okay, Harrison, I'll sort it out with Mrs Argyle. But this is an issue the police need to investigate at once."

Harrison's eyes widened and he kept staring at the toilet bowl, his mouth agape. Now even the butler was mad. The situation had likewise become too much for him, and he also considered the clogged toilet bowl a palpable threat. These thoughts now flashed through Harrison's frenzied mind. He quickly grabbed his bucket and plunger and left the room.

Beanstock had no choice; he was obligated to call the police. Truth be told, he would have preferred to wait for the documents to arrive from London, but this urgent matter was to be dealt with post-haste. He contemplated how he could manage to keep Mrs Argyle out of the whole troublesome ordeal. It would be challenging, to say the least. But she was already aware of the problem: he had pointed it out to her when he discovered increasingly more suspicious activities of the publisher. Nevertheless, he would do his best.

The butler made his way to the telephone in the hall, dialled the number of the small Parsley Field police station and soon heard the ringtone.

The receiver was picked up almost immediately and the Constable answered with a flustered yet earnest voice.

"Parsley Field Police Station, Constable Thomas

Devin Donegal speaking, Deputy Chief Officer, Inspector Richard Greenwood is currently unavailable, what do you have to report?"

Beanstock could see the Constable in his mind's eye. No doubt he had written down his superior's orders word for word, and was now rattling them down for every call. It was usually Miss Watson who tended to the activities at the police counter and thus answered all calls.

Beanstock hesitated for a moment. "Alright, Constable, where is the Inspector? It's extremely important."

Beanstock heard the man frenetically turning the pages of his notepad.

"The Inspector is attending a conference in London. What do you have to report?"

Beanstock rolled his eyes. "I have vital suspicions to report in the case of the two murdered women. The Inspector should be informed of them immediately."

"OK, so you have some suspicions. The Inspector is in Londo'... Oh, that's right – I already told you ... what do you have to report ...?" Constable Donegal realised he had already asked this question. Beanstock again heard the sound of pages turning in the Constable's notepad, at which point the butler became indignant.

"Constable, unless there is another option, it would be ideal if you came to the manor, so I could explain the situation to you."

Beanstock's suggestion was met by silence at the other end of the line and then the sound of Donegal clearing his throat.

"Well, uh", one could hear the policeman was trying to conjure up an appropriate response. "Okay, I guess I could come see you. It's extremely inconvenient for us that Miss Watson stayed home again due to her bad cough. You may already know about her bothersome cough, but nothing seems to help, absolutely nothing. And now our police station is left short-staffed because of it."

The frantic turning of pages could be heard.

"I guess I'll have to leave the station unattended now, although the Inspector will surely disapprove." The Constable was heard rifling through the pages of his notepad. "The Inspector instructed me to avoid unnecessary trips in the vicinity." With those words, the receiver was abruptly hung up.

Beanstock reached for his handkerchief to dry his forehead. He audibly sighed, squared his shoulders, tugged his jacket into place and went to the front door to await the policeman. After all, the journey surely wouldn't take too long.

It took a solid half hour.

To Beanstock's astonishment, the constable arrived by bicycle. The exertion was clearly visible on the policeman's face, since the occasional beer he had with his friend, Sean O'Donoghue, had already caused a visible bulge in his midriff. The old service bike had not been oiled for a long time and squeaked every time it was pedalled. Upon finally reaching the entrance, he clumsily dismounted and panted heavily as he leaned on the bicycle handlebars. He inhaled deeply and then gasped breathlessly: "The Inspector took the official car to London, of course. What do you have to report that is so urgent, Mr Beanstock?"

The butler unceremoniously took the bicycle from him and set it aside.

When he turned around, the Constable had already pulled out his notepad and a pencil, sharpened according to regulations. At that moment Harrison emerged from the front door carrying a broom. When he saw the Constable, he awkwardly scratched his head. In passing, he turned to the Constable and murmured sheepishly, "The toilet in the guest room is clogged."

Constable Donegal expressed his exasperation with pursed lips and bulging eyes.

"Mr Beanstock!" He was now hopping from one foot to the other. "What am I supposed to make of this? You called me all the way here because of a *clogged toilet*?! This is a waste of police resources, not to mention completely unacceptable."

Beanstock rolled his eyes.

"Of course this is not the only reason I summoned you. Will you please follow me inside now?" He gave the house servant a deprecating look, whereupon the latter busily started sweeping. On their way upstairs, the lord of the manor and his wife approached Beanstock and the Constable. "Beanstock, what on earth is the matter?" Sir Percival asked in amazement.

"Sir, I chanced upon some vital information which I intend to share with the police. Unfortunately, it expressly incriminates Milady's publisher. I had no other choice and hoped to act in your stead."

Beanstock then stopped and wondered whether it would have been more appropriate to inform his lordship beforehand.

Lady Fedora reassured him. "As you know, you have our implicit trust and I'm sure you did the right thing. We shall join you in a moment; that is if you don't mind, Constable?"

The policeman shook his head. When the small group had arrived at the publisher's guest room, Lady Fedora anxiously explained that she felt uneasy about entering her publisher's accommodation in his absence.

"I suppose it cannot be avoided, Darling", her husband stated, his curiosity clearly visible.

They entered the room. The butler began to explain the results of his detective work.

Donegal diligently wrote down everything the butler recounted, so as not to forget a single word.

Beanstock threw an anxious glance at Lady Fedora.

"Some days ago, I learned from a well-informed source that Van Horten is in all likelihood not the real name of your publisher, Milady. Moreover, I discovered that he once worked as a psychiatrist at the Bethlehem Royal Hospital for mentally ill persons before the war."

Lady Fedora turned pale.

"What are you trying to tell me? You can't be serious, Beanstock! Surely it's simply a case of mistaken identity!"

"Regrettably, I won't have solid evidence until a few days from now. Until then, let's assume it is indeed true. Which means Mr Van Horten recognised Miss Inga Hillman when he arrived at the manor. As Milady surely knows, Miss Emely Hillman was treated at Bethlehem Royal Hospital until her tragic death. I assume Mr Van Horten — let's stick to this name for now — felt threatened by something in his past. I can only surmise it had to do with Emely Hillman's death. But before he could be exposed, he decided to plot a vile murder, instead."

Sir Percival quickly grasped his wife's arm and sat her on the edge of the guest bed. She retrieved a handkerchief from her blouse pocket and excitedly fanned her face.

"But you don't actually have any evidence of this either, do you, Mr Beanstock?" she asked visibly distressed at this macabre turn of events.

"Lady Fedora, you certainly remember Miss Inga Hillman's excessive cigarette consumption. On the day of her death, the golden cigarette case disappeared without a trace. Since the coroner's diagnosis was inhalation of poison, I suspect Mr Van Horten exchanged the cigarettes in the case with the poison-laced cigarettes.

I am aware that Inspector Greenwood is also pursuing a lead concerning these cigarettes. The coroner suspected ricin which is colourless, odourless and literally tasteless. Dr Seeker knew of a discovery after the war, which involved containers of ricin and medical documents describing secret experiments on humans in an abandoned storeroom.

Van Horten did not have the opportunity to retrieve the cigarette case after the murder; Bernice took it the morning she found Miss Hillman's body. The maid must have observed something peculiar on the day of the reception. Perhaps she had witnessed the publisher tampering with the case. However, she had no idea at the time that the cigarettes had been tainted with poison. In all likelihood she then attempted to blackmail Van Horten. Which was a fatal mistake. On the day of the Inspector's interview, I witnessed a heated exchange between Bernice and Van Horten. The publisher knew that she also enjoyed smoking and therefore deliberately orchestrated her death. I found a burn mark on Bernice's garments, but no sign of any cigarettes. Van Horten must have taken the case after the girl's death. But as mentioned, I couldn't find it anywhere. All I found was a clogged toilet."

Constable Donegal looked up from his pad and cleared his throat.

"This sort of thing can happen even in the best families, Mr Beanstock."

The Constable, Sir Percival and Beanstock went into the small bathroom and for the second time that day a group of lay plumbers crouched over the toilet to examine its contents with great interest.

"When Harrison was busy clearing the clogged toilet, we found a large quantity of paper and crumbled cigarettes in it. Since the publisher doesn't smoke, the poisoned cigarettes sprung to mind again. He took the cigarette case after Bernice's death, dumped the rest of the cigarettes in the toilet and then got rid of the case."

"But my good Beanstock, where is the evidence? To be honest, I don't see the significance of a few cigarettes floating around in the toilet bowl!" Sir Percival rumbled.

"And", the Constable pointed out with a raised forefinger, "since the cigarettes have been floating in the toilet, the coroner won't be able to detect any poison."

"Well", Beanstock replied as he made his way to the chest of drawers and pulled it forward. He retrieved the black case and opened it.

"Do you see this? I'm almost certain the coroner will find poison after testing the contents of these vials. Not to mention the sachets of white powder, which he no doubt planted on Miss Hillman to distract attention from his crime, thus orchestrating her death as a cocaine overdose."

The butler handed the case to the Constable, whereupon he recalled the small vial he had previously taken out. He coughed slightly as he retrieved it from his pocket and put it back into the case.

The Constable shook his head.

"So… what is this so-called information you're waiting for? You mentioned that evidence will soon be available that'll verify Mr Van Horten's identity?" the Constable asked after skimming his notes.

"I expect that my source in London will send me the documents to prove that Emely Hillman also died from poisoning. And we will also have evidence that confirms Mr Van Horten had been working in Bedlam and conducted experiments on his patients."

Constable Donegal tucked his pencil into the side of his notepad.

"What you have told me constitutes sufficient grounds for an investigation. I'm going to call the Inspector in London immediately. Where is Mr Van Horten at the moment? I'll escort him to the police station for an interview until the Inspector arrives."

Everyone in the room looked at each other, visibly concerned.

"But we don't know where my publisher is. We've been searching for him since early this morning",

Lady Fedora replied.

"May I use your telephone, Milady?" the Constable asked with a slight bow. "And please ensure no one else sets foot in this room until the forensics team arrives."

Sir Percival nodded in agreement.

The Constable went downstairs to the hall and dialled a number. After a short time he was heard asking for Inspector Greenwood. It took a few moments before the Inspector answered. The Constable recited his notes to his superior. Shortly afterwards he hung up the phone and turned to the others awaiting his response.

"The Inspector is on his way. The forensics team will re-examine the room. I've been instructed to find Mr Van Horten. Do you have any idea where he might have gone?"

Beanstock explained to him that since the publisher's car was still in the garage, he could only get around on foot.

"He may also have gone to the station and taken the train", Beanstock surmised.

Constable Donegal was about to make his way to the station.

"Perhaps you'd better take the car. That is, if Sir Percival agrees …?" the butler suggested.

"Of course you may use our car as long as you need it, Constable"

The policeman accompanied the butler to the

garage. After a short time Gonzales was ready and eager to embark on another detective mission. He rubbed his hands determinedly.

"*El Asesino*, here we come, *Maldito*."

Gonzales drove the car out of the garage. Constable Donegal sat next to him in the front seat. Gonzales shot a strangely appraising glance at him. The policeman felt uncomfortable and nervously stroked his hair.

"Why aren't we going yet?"

"Señor, we certainly can't leave without Mr Beanstock?"

The back door was opened and the butler got in.

"You're not actually obligated to accompany us, Mr Beanstock", the Constable grumbled.

"I can take care of this on my own and, furthermore, the Inspector is asking for disclosure of your sources, Mr Beanstock."

Gonzales looked back over his shoulder and shrugged apologetically.

"No, I'm pleased to accompany you and be of assistance. As the saying goes: two heads are better than one."

The butler preferred to withhold the fact that he wanted to personally witness Van Horten's explanation. He ignored the policeman's reminder regarding the disclosure of his informants. He would have to come up with a viable explanation in the interim.

Their first destination was the train depot. As was his daily custom at this particular time, Mr Templar sat on the small bench in front of the station building while enjoying his tea. In response to the policeman's questions, he explained that no one had taken the train to London this morning and there would only be one other train departing at 6:00 this evening. Yes, he would be vigilant and notify the police station immediately.

Beanstock realised that the scandal would circulate around Parsley Field in no time, since the stationmaster had already been informed of the search warrant for Van Horten. The three gentlemen criss-crossed the surroundings for nearly an hour without so much as a trace. After half an hour, the first curious faces had appeared at the windows of the local pub, and a few minutes later the establishment had become unusually popular for this time of day. Beer-drinking groups occupied the bar counter and discussed the possible reasons regarding the search for the elegant London *upstart*.

Sean O'Donoghue commented on the *upstart* with a raised eyebrow and a clearing of the throat: many years ago, when he came to Parsley Field with his parents and settled there, the family had earned the moniker of the Dublin *upstarts*. But he refrained from making a comment. So many paying customers at this time of day guaranteed a welcome bonus for the *Jack O'Lantern* pub.

He grinned at the uptick in activity and began to sing a soft melody.

"Little Jack Horner
Sat in the corner
Eating a Christmas pie
He stuck in his thumb
And pulled out a plum and said
What a good boy
What a good boy
What a good boy am I!"

The search party led by Constable Donegal drove past the pharmacy and eventually made a right turn at the River Shirty. They pulled up to the hotel, but there was no sign of Van Horten there, either. Beanstock asked an unfamiliar young lady at the hotel reception desk for Mrs Partridge.

"Well, it's quite strange… This is the first time that Mrs Partridge hasn't shown up for work without any explanation. Our director Mr Divari was rather displeased this morning." She had a guilty expression on her face. Beanstock remembered his last encounter with Mrs Partridge at the hotel: he had gotten the distinct impression she didn't want to talk to him at all that day.

On their way back, they even searched the old convent ruins. Constable Donegal wanted to put the publisher on the most wanted list. After dropping the

Constable off at the police station, they drove home in silence. The forensics team vehicle was already parked in front of the mansion.

"What do you think, Señor? Where could the gentleman have disappeared to?"

Beanstock was silent, lost in thought. After Gonzales had parked the car in the garage, the butler disembarked with the distinct feeling of having overlooked something.

Gonzales grabbed a soft cloth and began to clean the windows.

"He has such a magnificent car and yet he just left it here. If he had taken it, he would have already been in France by now or *la maravillosa España*." The chauffeur whistled a quiet tune.

Beanstock looked at him in surprise.

"But of course! Why indeed would he leave such an expensive car here? You're a clever dick, Gonzales!"

Beanstock hastily left the garage. The chauffeur gazed after him in amazement.

"What in the world is a clever dick? It's not a swear word, is it?" he muttered.

In the meantime, the forensics team had finished their work in the manor and had once again turned the guest room upside down. Mrs Argyle groaned when she saw the room in complete disarray.

"And still no prospect of a new maid." She went down to the hallway where the butler was on the phone with the police station. Unfortunately, he did not get the desired information. The Inspector was en route and only expected to arrive that evening.

"Not only did he leave the suspicious vials here, but also his flashy car, Constable!" Beanstock remarked with a smile.

The Constable replied in astonishment: "But we already knew that, didn't we? What more is there to discuss?"

Beanstock hung up the phone without saying goodbye to the policeman. His mind was racing.

"Mr Beanstock, there's a letter in your office. It was delivered by courier while you were out."

The butler did not hear Mrs Argyle's last words. With a barely audible "Thank you", he headed for the office at lightning speed. He opened the door and there it was: a large, thick brown envelope with a white daisy in the middle. Beanstock smiled. He tore the envelope open with great anticipation. There were several yellowed sheets and a thin light green folder with a single sheet exhibiting fine penmanship and an illegible stamp at the bottom. The butler read the contents and then slowly raised his head. He pulled up his chair and sat down.

"This is certainly the last thing I would have expected", he whispered, the sheet trembling in his hands.

"I've never forgotten anything, not an action, not a name, not a face..."

It was dark except for a narrow band of light containing dancing pieces of fluff that shimmered beneath the closed door.

She gingerly raised her head and for a moment had no idea where she was. What on earth had happened?

A dull ache was throbbing behind her temples. Just like every morning, she had made a cup of tea, eaten a piece of toast and then set off to work. Wait, no, today was somehow different. Fragmented recollections of the morning flashed through her mind. It hadn't been a typical morning at all. Except that the tea had been ready for her when she entered the kitchen. She had thought how kind it was for George to prepare tea for her before making his rounds. The tea didn't taste particularly good, though. And then she became utterly exhausted.

No matter how hard she tried, she couldn't remember anything else. She attempted to stand up.

But she couldn't move a muscle and then she heard footsteps in the corridor.

Which corridor was the sound coming from? Where was she? What was this old, dingy room she was sitting in? It smelled like dust, dirt and mice. She was certain she heard the pattering of tiny paws. She strained her eyes while attempting to see. But it was too dark.

After her eyes had gotten accustomed to the darkness, she could only discern a few shadowy outlines in the room: a wardrobe, a chest of drawers and a table in the middle. She was sitting on a hard chair. Terror crept into her heart like a slowly slithering snake.

The door opened and a shadow slipped into the room.

Behind her back, someone pulled back the thick curtains on the window a bit, which accorded sufficient light to render the objects in the room more visible.

"Lies, lies, nothing but lies", a voice whispered from the back of her neck. Her scalp began to prickle. *"Not that you lied to me but that I no longer believe you – that is what has distressed me."*

The figure walked around in the room.

"Nietzsche was quoted as saying this in his book *Beyond Good and Evil*. Appropriate, don't you think? Take a look around, my dear. We can discuss your transgressions later."

230

The curtain was pulled back a little further, allowing fragments of light to penetrate the room. Then she heard the door shut. The sound of footsteps diminished and she breathed a sigh of relief. Although the voice was familiar, he had spoken very softly.

Upon surveying the room and now realising where she was, she started to tremble again. A doll was sitting nearby on what had once been a beautiful chest of drawers made of reddish cherrywood. It was a clown with orange-red hair and a grin on his painted face. It had been Emely's favourite doll. She recognised it immediately. She would never forget the happy little girl's laughter when she received this doll from her daddy.

Emely with her beautiful dark curls and delicate facial features. And next to the doll in the corner was the old doll's pram. The white laces, which now appeared torn, sad and dirty, were dangling downwards.

There was decay and dust everywhere. This was the Hillman children's playroom. She was in the Hillman's old mansion. But why was she here?

What was this wicked game being played with her? Her heart started to throb painfully.

Beanstock was still working his way through the closely written pages. According to the patient documents, Miss Emely Hillman had died of heart failure. It was a common cause of death and had been justified on account of her addled state, a weak heart and the administration of potent medication. As Beanstock had already expected, the death certificate was signed by Dr Richard McLean.

In addition to the death certificate, a list of the medications administered as well as a very interesting article from the August 1930 issue of The Times had been sent. Several former Cambridge University students were mentioned in an article and seen in a group photograph. Although the photo was very old and had since yellowed, the butler immediately recognised Van Horten, previously known as Richard McLean.

Students Kim Philby, Guy Burgess, Anthony Blunt, Donald and his brother Richard McLean and John Caircross congratulate their Dean Sir Reginald Barcley was written below the photo. This was sufficient proof.

However, if it turned out this proof was not sufficient to satisfy the Inspector, it would certainly be feasible to request documents from Cambridge, and Van Horten, alias McLean, would then be convicted accordingly. In all likelihood His Majesty's Secret Service would also take an interest in the case. Beanstock looked again at the official letter in the green folder.

"The poor girl", he whispered in dismay.

He had to take decisive action. When he entered

the kitchen area, the servants on hand at Parsley Manor were busy making preparations for the daily teatime. Beanstock gazed at the clock on the wall which had just struck 5:00 p.m. Teatime. Was it really so late? He went to the telephone and dialled the number of the *Rosebud* hotel. The receptionist answered immediately. Beanstock asked for Mrs Partridge and was informed as expected: nobody knew where she was, she had not reported for duty. The butler then called Mr Partridge at the post office.

"What are you playing at, Mr Beanstock? Why are you asking me when I last saw my wife? What exactly is that supposed to mean?"

The postman sounded agitated over the phone.

"I saw her this morning at home. Do you mind telling me what this is all about?" Beanstock excused himself, hung up and immediately dialled the number of the Winterbottoms' surgery.

The call remained unanswered for a while until Dr Timothy Winterbottom finally picked up the phone, apologised for the lengthy wait, explained that the reception was unstaffed today and asked the nature of his call. The butler hung up without a word, much to the consternation of the puzzled and annoyed doctor who returned to preparing a syringe to administer a long overdue vaccination to a quivering little boy named Charly. He would deal with his anger over the butler's atypical rudeness later,

Beanstock stood by the phone in contemplation.

Phillis had overheard everything in the kitchen and now joined him in the staff dining room.

"Is anything wrong with my mother, Sir? I overheard you speaking to my father."

She looked very worried and nervously fidgeted with her apron.

"Don't worry Phillis, I'm sure everything is just fine. Mrs Argyle!" He called loudly for the housekeeper as he was running out. She rushed out of the kitchen with a tray and looked at the butler in astonishment.

"Is anything wrong? You look pale, Mr Beanstock."

"Mrs Argyle, Isidora, I must leave at once. I hope it won't be too late. Please tend to the needs of Milord and Milady. I'll take the car. Call the police station and send the Constable to the Hillman's old mansion. I think I know where to find Mr Van Horten."

The cook's rosy face appeared in the door to the kitchen. She was wielding a large wooden spoon from which some reddish jam was spilling onto her apron. It was the season to make jam at Parsley Manor. The sticky stain around Mrs Porkpie's mouth made Mrs Argyle heave an audible sigh.

The butler suddenly bolted through the back door to the kitchen garden. Mortecai, who was about to inspect whether he could glean something from the kitchen during his afternoon rounds, barely managed to get out of the butler's path with an indignant meow. Beanstock ran into the garage.

"Gonzales, hurry up, we must go to the Hillman's old mansion immediately."

"Si, si, Señor, I am ready."

The chauffeur didn't take the time to don his good jacket, but instead jumped into the Bentley as he was, shirt sleeves rolled up and engine oil on his face, and revved the engine.

"Do you think we'll find the missing gentleman there?"

"I suspect as much and surely hope we won't be too late."

The car shot out of the driveway. Leaning on his broom, Harrison watched the two men as they sped away, shaking his head uncomprehendingly.

"Wonder what could be the matter now... Slowly but surely this mansion is turning into a madhouse", he muttered. The astonished faces of Sir Percival and Lady Fedora appeared at the salon window. Harrison turned to them and shrugged his shoulders.

At that moment Mr. Partridge, the postman, turned the corner on his bike. He stopped beside the house servant and watched the car as it sped off. Phillis and Mrs Argyle appeared in the doorway of the main entrance. The kitchen maid ran to her father and hugged him.

"What is going on, my child?" Mr Partridge asked his daughter, who looked at him in confusion.

"The hotel staff told me that your mother didn't make it to work this morning. And then Mr Beanstock asked me if I knew her whereabouts."

Mrs Argyle reassuringly put her hand on his shoulder.

"Mr Beanstock suspects Milady's publisher is at the Hillman's old mansion. I have no idea how this could have anything to do with your wife."

The postman did not say a word. His mind was racing. He knew about his wife's connection to the Hillmans.

He turned his bicycle around, shouted to Mrs Argyle to look after Phillis and dashed off as if he had taken leave of his senses.

Lady Fedora stepped out of the house, put her arm around Phillis's shoulders and spoke soothingly to her.

"A cup of tea will do you good now, my child."

She winked at the housekeeper. Mrs Argyle nodded in agreement. Junior slipped out just before the door slammed shut, barking loudly, and ran across the courtyard long after the car had disappeared. Realising he was too late, he lay down impassively in the driveway.

Mortecai watched his favourite adversary from the safety of the kitchen garden wall. An astute observer might have thought the tomcat was grinning. His velvety paw smoothed his well-groomed white beard in amusement and his bushy tail performed a lithesome dance.

Mrs Partridge had tried in vain to loosen the bonds, but they had not budged at all. By now her joints were aching terribly.

She heard the sound of footsteps in the corridor.

What time could it be? She had completely lost track.

It seemed to be growing dark outside. The door opened. Someone placed an object on the centre of table, and then she heard a match being lit. The inside of the room brightened and she finally had a better view. But at that moment she would have far preferred to continue being kept in the dark. The man walked across the room, singing a soft melody.

"Little Jack Horner
Sat in the corner
Eating a Christmas pie

He stuck in his thumb
And pulled out a plum and said
What a good boy
What a good boy am I!"

Mrs Partridge could not believe her eyes.

"Simon, my boy, what are you doing here? Please untie me!"

"Tsk, tsk, tsk, my dear mother, my caring attentive

MOTHER!" He overaccentuated the term 'mother'.

"Do you remember the time I was sick? I was six years old then and suffered from a terrible whooping cough. You used to sing that children's song to me. Do you remember?"

Simon now stood right in front of his mother and spat the last words into her face: "*What a good boy am I*! I am a good boy, aren't I, MOTHER?"

Beads of sweat appeared on his forehead and he looked around anxiously.

"How did that come about again? Oh yes: Emely fell into a depression after her parents died and her aunt had nothing better to do than take her to a mental hospital. People must never find out about such things, don't you agree? How embarrassing this would have been! To make it worse, she became a patient of this mad doctor, or should I be more specific, 'that mad physician, Dr Richard McLean'. She was just another guinea pig to him. He sent her to her death with his poison and made it appear as though she died of heart failure. What a very evil man he is, don't you agree? And I had to do away with him, of course. Just as I did away with Emely's evil aunt earlier, you know what I mean? Yes, I'm sure you know everything."

"Simon, what in the world are you talking about, I had no clue."

"Nothing but lies, your lies will be the death of you!"

Simon turned Mrs Partridge's armchair towards the table so she could see the objects beside the flickering candlelight: a shimmering golden cigarette case, a wooden box with a slightly faded dark red rose on the lid and a pile of letters bound together with a green bow.

Mrs Partridge recognised the letters.

"Where did you get those letters from?"

"You had certainly hidden them very well. But perhaps you ought to have burned them, instead. Oh, what a curse it is that old people have the compulsion to hoard everything they've ever owned, don't you agree?"

"Simon, you don't understand. Let me explain..."

"You can't justify your actions to me with your explanations. You admitted Emely was taken to this monster at the mental hospital when she became pregnant. You allowed the baby to be taken away from her after it was born and you turned a blind eye to her death. Did she perhaps die of a broken heart? No! She died a miserable death from being poisoned. How must her last hours have played out? Alone, without her child, without comfort and in excruciating pain?

You allowed dear Aunt Agatha and Dr McLean to put the child in your arms before you walked away. The good aunt was very pleased. She had sufficient means now and there were no Hillman descendants who might attempt to lay claim to the money.

Priscilla was lucky enough to escape to safety early on. But you also betrayed my Aunt Priscilla. I wish she'd have never come back to this place. She'd still be alive now and so would little Bernice. Yes, you have her on your conscience as well. When I found the letters you received from Aunt Agatha and that doctor, I put two and two together. And dealt with dear Auntie, and then Dr McLean as I saw fit. Would you like to say hello to him now, Mother?"

Simon walked to the door to open it and then turned his mother's armchair towards the door. A rope was suspended from the banister and disappeared downwards. Simon pushed the armchair slightly closer to the door so that Mrs Partridge could see the publisher's head dangling from the noose.

She closed her eyes at the gruesome spectacle.

"Perhaps I wouldn't have noticed that he was a guest at Parsley Manor, but I definitely wanted to meet my Aunt Priscilla, which is why I stood in front of her window that night. She was so beautiful. I'm sure Emely was also very pretty. I returned to the mansion on the day of the reception. And I noticed you in the bushes. You wanted to see her too, didn't you? You nearly spotted me. Then I saw him; he was standing there with his smug, arrogant smile on his ugly face, feeling safe and secure. I recognised him immediately, for I had thoroughly done my research, you know. When I completed my nursing degree in London back then, I had a lot of time to devote to it.

How unfortunate I realised too late that he would hurt Priscilla. I didn't expect him to do her any harm."

"But Simon, I was only trying to help. How awful it would have been if you'd been sent to an orphanage!"

"Shut up!" Simon grumbled angrily as he menacingly approached the armchair.

The Bentley raced around the corners with impressive speed. Gonzales focused on the road while Beanstock gripped the seat cushions, just to be on the safe side. Ten minutes later they had reached the driveway of the old Hillman mansion. It was already the onset of sunrise.

Foreboding clouds promised a storm. The first flashes of lightning could be seen in the distance while claps of thunder resonated in the background.

The wrought-iron gate hung askew on its hinges and the path to the house was overgrown with grass and weeds. Dry leaves were swirling around in the approaching wind.

The two gentlemen stepped out of the vehicle.

"Do you have a torch in the car, Gonzales?" the butler asked, looking up apprehensively at the mansion's dark façade.

Gonzales opened the boot and retrieved a torch from the toolbox. Upon a brief inspection to ensure it still functioned properly, he nodded in satisfaction and handed it to the butler.

The two men slowly and cautiously approached the house.

"All that's missing is the screeching of an owl, straight out of one of those horror films", Gonzales whispered into the butler's ear. As though right on cue, the gruesome screeching of an owl could be heard. The two looked at each other, their eyebrows raised.

Gonzales bent down briefly and picked up an object that had caught his attention. He held a thick branch in his hands; a short check of it satisfied him and he followed the butler. Beanstock stopped.

"What do you intend to do with that club?" he whispered.

"*Nunca se sabe*, Señor Beanstock", he replied in the same low voice.

"I beg your pardon?"

"*Maldito*, you never know."

"Why didn't you say so in the first place?"

The two men proceeded carefully towards the mansion. Upon arriving at the front door, Beanstock listened for movement inside. No sounds could be heard. Beanstock pushed the door open which was only ajar. The creaking of the old door made him stop in his tracks. He listened, but was met by total silence.

When they reached the hall, Beanstock slowly lit up the room with the torch. They tiptoed to the stairs to get an upward view. But before they arrived at the stairs, they heard a creaking sound similar to ropes from the rig of a ship swaying in the wind. Beanstock shone his torch up to the first floor. Gonzales clamped his hand over his mouth in horror at the macabre sight of legs and feet – in very expensive handmade shoes as Beanstock surmised – dangling from the ceiling.

"My guess is they're genuine Mufforts & Portermans, a respectable company", he whispered.

When light of the torch exposed a face, they recognised Van Horten. His eyes were grossly enlarged and his complexion had taken on a bluish tinge.

At that moment they heard singing that originated from the first floor. They tiptoed step by step to the source of the noise without making a sound.

They heard fragments of conversation behind a door. When they drew nearer, Beanstock recognised the voices. What the two men overheard confirmed the butler's suspicions: it was a murderer's confession.

All of a sudden the door was flung open. A beam of light illuminated the corridor. Gonzales had quickly moved into the shadows on the other side of the door while Beanstock pressed himself close to the wall on the right. They heard chair legs scraping across the floor and the sound of sobbing after Mrs Partridge had discovered the slain publisher. They then continued listening to the murderer's confessions, thus putting the final pieces of the puzzle together for Beanstock.

When Simon angrily turned to Mrs Partridge and shouted right in her face to be quiet, the butler wordlessly communicated the next course of action to Gonzales. He glanced at him encouragingly and silently moved his lips while counting down from three. Then they both jumped on Simon, knocking him down to the floor. During the scuffle that ensued, both Simon and the butler were groping around for Gonzales' club. Finally, the pair of them was able to overpower Simon. The young man lay on the floor, his face beet red and contorted with anger. Gonzales tore some curtain tape from the window curtains with which he bound Simon's hands until he could no longer move.

When Beanstock had finally freed Mrs Partridge, police cars could be heard approaching in the distance. Beanstock was relieved at the sound and closed his eyes. Mrs Partridge knelt beside her son and sobbed quietly.

"What have you done, Simon? I only acted with the best intentions. I couldn't do anything to help Emely, but I could at least save you from the clutches of that horrible aunt. She would have left you with that doctor and he would have killed you, too. You're still my Simon, aren't you?"

"I have never been your Simon", the young man on the floor hissed and turned away.

When the sound of feet running up the stairs was heard and the flickering glow of torches became visible, Beanstock turned his gaze to the table. He almost tenderly opened the small wooden box and saw the cheap trinkets Bernice had stashed there. He stroked the items that had meant so much to her, and also caught sight of the gold cigarette case, from which a scent of vanilla wafted through the room.

"Shalimar", Beanstock whispered.

Inspector Greenwood appeared with the Constable and several uniformed policemen he had brought from London as back-up. The forensics team set about their work, and Van Horten, alias McLean, was taken down and brought to the coroner's office.

Mrs Partridge was severely stricken. Dr Winterbottom was called to the scene and admitted her to the nearest hospital to recover. Her husband, who had arrived at the same time as the Inspector, accompanied her. He could not yet fathom the full extent of what had happened.

Beanstock retrieved the document from the green folder in his pocket and handed it to the Inspector.

Dr Winterbottom also closely examined the birth certificate dated December 1929. The birth of a healthy boy named Simon Patrik Hillman had been recorded on the certificate. Pale and with teary eyes, he returned the certificate to the Inspector. He had not only lost his best nurse, but above all, he was shaken by the fact his own son had worked by his side for years without being any the wiser. But even Simon had no knowledge of his father's identity. What's more, the boy had never been interested in his identity.

Nobody would ever know exactly when these issues brought the onset of his psychosis or when his anger intensified to such an extreme degree. He was immediately transferred to London where he would await his trial. In all likelihood he would be spared the death penalty since his defence lawyer relied on a psychiatrist's report according to which he was legally insane and had pathological proclivities. If the court ruled in his favour, he would serve the rest of his life in a psychiatric institution for dangerous criminals.

"What a terrible story. How can so many lives become so derailed in such a short time." Lady Fedora sighed as she leaned back in her comfortable armchair in the salon and gazed into an uncertain distance. Beanstock poured a cup of tea and handed it to Milady.

"If I may say so, Milady, the trigger was Aunt Agatha Eugenie Hillman. Although it's futile to speculate 'if only…' in retrospect, if this evil woman had not taken Emely Hillman to that hospital, all those poor people might still be alive. Even wicked Aunt Agatha."

Life at Parsley Manor resumed its usual leisurely pace. The servant Harrison was finally allowed to fix the stubborn toilet blockage in the blue room. Gardener Mr Herringbone shook his head upon reading about the castor-oil plant in his botany book. Mrs Porkpie lived up to her reputation and was making jam non-stop.

The kitchen maid Phillis was slowly recovering from the shock due to the discovery that her brother was not actually her biological brother.

Filomena Arbuckle, Lady Fedora's maid, was planning a long-awaited vacation and was the least unnerved of anyone in the Parsley Manor household.

After much hesitation, the housekeeper hired a young girl named Elizabeth Trilby. She hailed from London and came highly recommended. The ensuing weeks would determine whether she was a perfect fit for Parsley Manor.

Mrs Isidora Argyle was no longer haunted by her dubious past since Beanstock had adroitly managed to keep her out of the Inspector's investigations. He staunchly refused to reveal the identity of his informants, the nature of Mrs Argyle's former activities, or the Daisy-Chain organisation. Inspector Greenwood finally gave up being upset about the situation and accepted Beanstock's stoicism.

Supporting documents were again provided through legal channels and in part confiscated by His Majesty's Secret Service. Dr McLean, his brother and a group of Cambridge students were investigated on suspicion of espionage.

Mr Beanstock looked forward to reading his mystery novels and hoped he could from now on merely be an observer of the written crimes therein. In the evening he sat in his comfortable room where the atmosphere was filled with the scent of blossoming roses and spicy mint thanks to the open window. He was holding the newest mystery novel by his favourite author Agatha Christie: *A Murder is Announced*.

"Miss Marple is investigating again with her unrivalled flair for human tragedies", the butler mused with a satisfied smile.

For a brief moment, his gaze wandered into the distance. A bit of excitement was in fact very refreshing. He was well-pleased, knowing this would not be the last case to be solved.

Something about me

I live and work in Magdeburg. Great Britain has been a dream destination for me for a long time. That's why my stories take place in this wonderful country.

This is the first book in the Beanstock series that I am publishing in English. Ten books in this cozy crime series have now been published.
In my second cozy crime „Barrington" I tell the story from the perspective of a Scottish pub landlord, who works as a hobby detective.

My fantasy youth book series „Peter Scott and the Lions of England" takes place in a fantastic world among London, Edinburgh and Cardiff. Young Peter realizes that not everything is as it seems.

I hope you enjoy my story.

For more Information you can find me at:

https://awbenedict.de/shop